"So how are we going to amuse ourselves, stuck out here at sea?" Sloan asked.

Cassidy flashed him a secret half-smile over the rim of her glass. "I would have thought that was obvious. We're going to be lovers."

Sloan choked on his champagne and Cassidy robustly pounded him on his back in a way he remembered from their youth.

"You've certainly become more direct. I like that in a woman," he gasped.

"I'm glad," Cassidy said. "So here's how it's going to play out. Ground rules: anything goes."

He stepped toward her. "I'm liking it so far."

She moved in so close, he could feel her body heat and smell her sultry fragrance. "It gets better." Her voice was a sexy purr. Not only did the hair on his arms rise, everything male sprang to instant and rapt attention.

"It's going to be the best sex you ever had," Cassidy said.

WICKED NIGHT GAMES

Praise for the sizzling erotic romances of

KATHLEEN LAWLESS

A HARD MAN TO LOVE

"A highly erotic page-turner."

—*Fallen Angel Reviews*

"Hot sex and spunky characters. . . . A keeper."

—*Fresh Fiction*

"A real keeper. . . . The love scenes are passionate and erotic."

—*Romance Junkies*

UNTAMED

"Full of wit and charm . . . highly entertaining. Full of adventure, romance, and daring-do . . . imagine Nancy Drew meets *Sex and the City*!"

—*Roundtable Reviews*

"Kathleen Lawless's story is fresh. . . . The dialogue is snappy and unique and the sex is riveting."

—*Romance Junkies*

"The growing relationship between the fully developed lead couple makes for a wonderful, heated tale."

—*The Best Reviews*

UNMASKED

"Passionate and erotic. . . . Readers looking for steamy, sensual scenes will love it."

—*Roundtable Reviews*

"Lawless weaves romance, intrigue, and excitement into an impressive tapestry. Do not miss this book."

—*Romance Reviews Today*

"An amusing, spirited, adventurous tale."

—*Romantic Times*

"A sensual read that will keep you spellbound until the very end."

—*Romance Junkies*

TABOO

"An engaging erotic romance . . . an entertaining tale."

—*Midwest Book Review*

". . . filled with erotic interludes."

—*A Romance Review*

Also by Kathleen Lawless

A Hard Man to Love

Untamed

Unmasked

Taboo

Wicked Night Games

KATHLEEN LAWLESS

POCKET BOOKS
New York London Toronto Sydney

POCKET BOOKS, a division of Simon & Schuster, Inc.
1230 Avenue of the Americas, New York, NY 10020

This book is a work of fiction. Names, characters, places, and incidents are products of the author's imagination or are used fictitiously. Any resemblance to actual events or locales or persons, living or dead, is entirely coincidental.

ISBN-13: 978-0-7394-8164-6

POCKET and colophon are registered trademarks of Simon & Schuster, Inc.

Manufactured in the United States of America

For all those who read *A Hard Man to Love*
and requested Sloan's story,
this one's for you.

Acknowledgments

Special thanks to fellow author Nancy Warren, who always makes time for our spectacular and inspiring writing retreats.

Wicked Night Games

Chapter One

"You don't recognize me, do you?"

Sloan Hardt gave the redheaded beauty his sexiest smile: the tilted head, the frank blue-eyed interest, and the "come keep me warm" crooked half grin. "Should I?"

"We went to school together."

"What school?" Sloan challenged, convinced she was mistaken. He never would have forgotten such a looker.

"West Bend High."

"Apparently I owe you a drink and an apology, Miss . . . ?" He waited expectantly, having already checked out her unadorned ring finger.

She met his gaze, her eyes the color of warm sherry. "I think I'll keep you waiting a little longer for that. See if it comes to you."

"That would be cruel beyond words. What are you drinking?"

"Champagne, of course. What else at a wedding?"

"You're here for a wedding? What a coincidence. Me, too."

"It's no coincidence, Sloan Hardt. We're here for the same wedding." Miss Red turned and sashayed away, leaving him with his mouth hanging open as she greeted his brother. Luckily, he could hear every word.

"Steele, when do I get to meet your wife?"

"As soon as I find her, I'll do the honors. Since she's pregnant, she's always in the bathroom."

After the redhead left, Steele went over to Sloan with a grin. "Jeez, man, pull up your jaw. I know she looks good, but—"

"Who is she?"

"Are you kidding me?" He cocked his thumb toward the departing redhead. "Little Cassidy Ferrill."

"*Fatty* Ferrill?"

"Be kind. She had a serious crush on you, man."

"What the hell is she doing on our parents' wedding cruise?"

"If you ever went to visit Gramps, you'd know that Cassidy's mother is his current squeeze."

Sloan let out a low whistle. "Go, Gramps, go."

"Yep. Louise Ferrill has given him a whole new lease on life."

"A whole new reason to get out of bed in the morning. Or better yet, stay there."

Steele punched him on the forearm. "Pretty sad state of affairs when our grandfather has a better love life than you do."

"Cut me some slack. You know I've been busy building the house and running Black Creek Ranch."

"I also know you need to get laid. I'd go talk nice to Cassidy, if I were you."

"For once, big brother, I am about to heed your advice."

It took him a while to hunt her down. A rancher, he wasn't used to crowds the way Steele was. It seemed like Angel and Rake, their parents, had invited everyone they knew to witness their rekindled love, making his progress slow as people he barely recognized stopped him constantly. Watching his folks across the room, he had to say they sure looked happy, and he felt a sudden, unaccustomed flash of envy. Ever since Steele had married Montana, and Rake and Angel had rediscovered true love, it felt as if everyone was paired up except him. He wasn't accustomed to being on the outside.

If memory served, Cassidy had never been much for crowds, either, so he took the hunt out onto the ship's promenade deck. Up-deck he spotted a flash of red hair shimmering in the sun and sped up his pace, careful not to spill the champagne he'd picked up on the way. As if she sensed his pursuit, Cassidy turned and waited for him.

"I bear champagne and an apology. Shame on me for not knowing who you were."

She dipped her fingers in the champagne and spinked them playfully his way. "Double shame."

His grin widened. "I should be punished."

"Spanked, perhaps," she said in a way that sent blood surging to his loins. This was a whole different Cassidy from his memories.

"To getting reacquainted." He clinked the rim of his glass to hers. "It's wonderful to see you again. I hear we're practically related."

Cassidy might have changed physically, but her smile still lit up her face. "It's great to see my mom so happy. She loves having James to fuss over, and he treats her like gold."

"She deserves that," Sloan said. Cassidy's father had not been a nice man, not to Cassidy or to her mother. "So how are we going to amuse ourselves, stuck out here at sea for days on end?"

Cassidy flashed him a half smile over the rim of her glass. "I would have thought that was obvious. We're going to be lovers."

As Sloan choked on his champagne, Cassidy robustly pounded on his back in a way he remembered from their youth.

"You've certainly become direct. I like that in a woman," he said through a gasp.

"I'm glad," Cassidy said. "So here's how it's going to play out. Ground rules: anything goes."

He stepped toward her. "I'm liking it so far."

She moved in so close, he could feel her body heat and

smell her sultry fragrance. "It gets better." Her voice was a sexy purr. Not only did the hair on his arms rise, everything male sprang to instant and rapt attention.

"It's going to be the best sex you ever had. Feeling warm and fuzzy from the wedding, you might start to think it's more. It won't be. So right up front, I'm telling you that once the ship gets back to port, we walk away in separate directions. No regrets. No false promises. Just happy memories. Agreed?"

He frowned. "There has to be a catch."

"Why?"

It seemed silly to say "because of what happened all those years ago." He cleared his throat. "One thing Gramps taught us was, if a thing looks too good to be true, it likely is."

She walked her fingers teasingly up his forearm. "Do I look too good to be true?" The brush of her fingertips, the whisper of her breath, had Sloan's impulses screaming, Who cares?

He blew out a breath. "You've obviously given this some thought."

She glanced up at him through her eyelashes. "I most certainly have."

Sloan knew he'd always had the golden touch with women; they fell into his lap like juicy, ripe fruit. Even so . . . "A shipboard fling?"

"No fantasy is forbidden on the Fantasy Cruise."

Mmmmm . . . Sloan could definitely weave a few fantasies about Cassidy. "How do we get started?"

"Like this." She plucked the empty flute from his hand,

set the glasses on a table, wound her arms around his neck, and pressed against him.

Sloan's arms encircled her with an unerring confidence, pulling her near. It had been way too long since he'd been this close to a woman. Especially one who felt this right in his arms.

At the first touch of her, the first taste of her, the years flew back, confusing his senses. Cassidy had been everybody's pal and nobody's sweetheart, a stand-in for his prom date who was home with the measles. And because he'd been selfish and shallow, he'd toyed with her emotions. Was it now her plan to toy with his?

Cassidy had waited a lifetime for this moment—step one in making Sloan fall for her—and she kept her eyes wide open for his kiss.

It didn't disappoint. His lips were soft at first, firm, shaping themselves to hers with tiny nibbles that promised great things to follow. He didn't try to force his tongue down her throat, but let her set the pace as her lips opened of their own accord, her tongue instinctively seeking his.

Cassidy felt as if the well of pent-up feelings inside of her drained into Sloan, leaving her empty. She clutched his shoulders as her body melted into him and then, like a miracle, she felt a surge of renewed energy. As if he took what she offered, doubled it, and refilled her wellspring.

The boy next door had turned into one fine specimen of a man. And he was going to fall in love with her so fast, he wouldn't know what hit him.

His hands were everywhere, stroking her hair, tracing her shape, cupping her behind and pulling her close. She made tiny murmurs of approval at what he was doing, the way he made her feel. She rubbed her breasts against his chest, pretending no barrier of clothing separated them, impatient for the heady sensation of skin on skin.

She felt him hard against her and tilted her pelvis, seeking his heat.

"God, Cassidy." His breathing was ragged as he dragged his mouth from hers and she could feel his heart racing. Or was that hers?

"A promising start." She smoothed her hair with unsteady hands and turned to face the sea, gripping the railing, reminding herself she needed to keep a level head.

"Wait till you see what I can do for an encore." Sloan moved in close, but not in a greedy, grasping way. First she felt the heat of his body, followed by the whisper of his breath. He swept her hair aside with a touch as light as the breeze, then tongued the sweet spot on the side of her neck.

Cassidy exhaled and clutched the railing tight as her head swayed, like a flower accepting the sun's loving warmth. There was no reason not to enjoy the sex while she taught Sloan a lesson.

His teasing tongue barely hinted at other delights he was capable of delivering, his gentleness confusing her overwhelmed senses. Staring out at the vast, blue ocean, she still couldn't believe she was here, in the arms of Sloan Hardt, about to embark on a sexual adventure with the ultimate payoff.

"We could go to my cabin." Was that her speaking so boldly, a boldness guaranteed to intrigue Sloan?

"I like it here," Sloan murmured against her skin. "Fresh ocean air. Sunshine."

"Anyone might see us."

"Who?" He slid down the spaghetti straps of her flouncy sundress, then followed the front edging and slid his middle fingers beneath, caressing the soft swell of her breasts, seeking the rapt attention of her cresting nipples.

The brush of his fingertips against that responsive flesh sent a sensation darting down to nest at the top of her thighs, and she gasped at the flash flood of desire. "Sloan, I—"

"Ssshhh. . . ." Subtly his fingers worked their magic on her breasts, his mouth hot and wet against her neck. She shifted her weight from side to side, trying to ease the increasing ache between her thighs. This wasn't the way she'd imagined it at all. He wasn't supposed to make her feel this much, this fast. She was supposed to have him groveling with lust.

His erection was hard against her bottom. "God, you are sweet." He reached around and pressed his palm to her pelvis. "I can feel your heat."

Let him think she was out of control; putty in his hands. "You make me hot."

"And wet. Do I make you wet?"

She nodded wordlessly.

"Turn around and face me."

She hoped her legs would hold her as she let go of the rail and turned inside the circle of his arms.

"Did you mean what you said? That anything goes?" He nudged one knee beneath her full skirt, pressed it to that aching, pulsing central core, and applied a divine pressure.

She moaned softly.

"Ride me." Sloan pivoted his knee from side to side and increased the pressure.

Cassidy gripped his shoulders and angled her body against his, moving with him and against him, leaning into him, then back.

When his clever fingers tweaked her nipples, her breath caught from the force of her desire. Her world spun out of control, into a place where nothing existed save Sloan and the way he was igniting foreign sensations, urging her to behave in unfamiliar ways, a prisoner to her newfound sensuality.

He read her body's response, matching her as she increased the pace. He kissed her face, her cheeks, her lips, her jaw, then finally surrendered his mouth to hers.

She inhaled him, devoured him, intent only on the much-needed release her body demanded, on the sudden, unexpected rush that made everything inside her shudder out of control, with Sloan's secure arms absorbing the impact, holding her close.

"Good girl." Sloan's smile made her heart flip as he lifted the straps of her dress back into place, seconds before his mother rounded the corner

"Sloan, Cassidy. I see you two have caught up with each other."

"You could say that." Sloan's voice was husky and Cassidy

quickly stepped in front of him to conceal his still-aroused state.

"It's almost time for the rehearsal, so I'm rounding everyone up."

"I'd think that you and Dad would be old hands after all these years, and wouldn't need a run-through."

"It's not your father I'm worried about," Angel said drily. "You, on the other hand, are as difficult as you ever were."

"Hey, I'm the easygoing one. Steele's the one who lived up to his name."

"Steele's soon to make me a grandmother," Angel said serenely. "While you seem as unsettled as ever."

"Unsettled? I'm building myself a house. Why am I suddenly a black sheep?" Sloan wished they weren't having this conversation in front of Cassidy.

Angel plucked a long red hair from his shoulder. "Just a gentle reminder that you're not getting any younger."

"I feel younger, now that I've run into Cassidy." He made an ushering gesture. "Lead the way. We're right behind you."

"No detours," Angel said. "I want my wedding to be perfect."

"Don't worry about Sloan, Angel. I'll keep him in check," Cassidy said.

"It's high time someone did."

Why did women make such a big deal about weddings? His father didn't seem nearly as intense as his mother had since the big announcement.

Dutifully, he took his place next to Steele and Rake near the front of the onboard chapel. Standing next to Steele's pregnant wife, Montana, was Cassidy's mother, Louise.

Tall, elegant, and silver-haired, Gramps, with Angel on his arm, proceeded from the back of the chapel to the front where Steele hummed Mendelsohn's "Wedding March" under his breath.

"You sure this rascal deserves a second chance?" Gramps said, to a smattering of laughter from those watching.

"He's your son," Angel said. "I figure if Louise can handle an old reprobate like you, I can handle Rake."

Sloan laughed and elbowed Steele, suddenly suffused with happy sentimentality. Family could be a pain sometimes, but they were a good pain.

"I expect he's learned his lesson," Gramps said.

Sloan sent a cocky look Cassidy's way and winked. She flushed a becoming pink, emphasizing the perfect porcelain cast of her complexion. Her full lips curved in a beguiling smile and her red-gold hair swung about her shoulders in soft waves.

His gaze never leaving hers, he pressed his lips together suggestively, revealing only the tip of his tongue.

She opened her lips and slowly traced them, emphasizing the glistening, moist pink within. Sloan imagined those hot wet lips on his cock and inwardly groaned. It was a damn good thing Steele was in charge of the ring; he only had to stand still and try not to embarrass himself.

He got no help from Cassidy. Out of sight of the others,

she inserted her index finger between her lips, circled it with her tongue several times, then plunged it into her mouth and slowly withdrew it, only to slide it back inside and pull on it like a sweet, melting popsicle.

Sloan blew out a breath. Just wait till he got her alone!

Chapter Two

"Isn't Angel beautiful?" Cassidy whispered to her mom.

"There's nothing like a wedding," Louise whispered back, dabbing at her eye. "I can't wait till it's your turn."

Cassidy cocked a glance to where James stood near Angel. "Maybe you'll beat me down the aisle. Why is James giving her away? He's the father of the groom."

"She was originally going to have the two boys give her away. Then James said that she was just like a daughter to him and . . ." She broke off with an apologetic sniff.

"Hey, even if my father was still alive, he wouldn't be the one on my arm on the big day."

Louise squeezed her arm extra tight.

Cassidy tried to picture Sloan as the anxious groom, but he was a solo act. He always had been. It was a role that suited him, the last of the lone riders; even the way he stood slightly apart from his brother and his father. The Hardt men were all individuals, each larger than life, each playing by his own rules.

Rake, the professional gambler who operated a Las Vegas casino, had passed that gambling bug to Steele. Sloan had made his own way, choosing to work the land—which was probably just as much of a gamble, though she doubted he saw it that way.

Her heart gave a leap as he turned her way, his gaze melting her insides. After the rehearsal would come her intimate interlude with Sloan, and nervousness battled excitement within her. If their earlier escapades on deck were any indicator, it should be simple to make Sloan fall madly for her.

The rehearsal was agony to Sloan, seeming to drag on forever. Cassidy was so sexy and beautiful, he couldn't concentrate on his surroundings. He kept envisioning her naked, her glorious hair spread out over his pillow, as he planned all the different ways he'd make love to her. Slow, then fast. Then slow again; he almost heard her screaming his name, begging for release.

When they were growing up, he'd never in a million years imagined her as a sexy temptress. She'd been funny Cassidy Ferrill, a homely lump with glasses, bad skin, and features that didn't quite fit her face. He'd dated her best friend, so he'd seen her lots.

Yet suddenly, it was as if he was seeing her for the first time.

He exhaled heavily. How much longer? When the rehearsal was finally over, he was so horny he was ready to pounce. And then she was in front of him, all soft and glowing, her key pressed into his palm.

"Give me half an hour, okay?"

No! He wanted to beat his chest and drag her off.

"Sure." What was she up to now? The old Cassidy wouldn't have been up to anything; he wasn't so sure of this new, sexy, confident model. They'd grown up on neighboring ranches, almost like brother and sister till they hit puberty and he'd discovered *girls.* Girls who liked him as much as he liked them. Cassidy's friend, Janine, had been the prize, the girl every guy wanted but Sloan got. And one fateful night, while Janine sat home with the measles, she'd insisted he take Cassidy to the prom.

He shouldn't have kissed Cassidy that night, letting her think he liked her. How was he to know that, suffused with guilt, she would tell Janine everything? It was the end of the three of them hanging out together.

"Where's Louise, Gramps?" He slid onto the bar stool next to his grandfather and ordered a Corona, cocking an inquiring eye at James's half-empty beer glass.

"Said she needed some time."

"Cassidy told me the same thing." He rubbed his thumb over the condensation on the outside of the bottle. "Weird things, weddings."

"They sure do seem to get the ladies all worked up."

"What do you reckon they mean when they say they need time, anyway?"

"That, my boy, is one of the many mysteries of the fairer sex."

"Don't you have them figured out yet, at your advanced age?"

"I'm lots wiser than when your grandma was alive. I've learned to say 'yes, dear' even when I don't understand the question." He laughed a secret laugh that made Sloan smile. "Cassidy turned out to be a real looker, didn't she? Just like her mom."

"Yeah. You see her much up at the ranch?"

"She comes by from time to time."

"She ever ask about me?'

"Not as I recall. Why?"

"No reason." He indicated the half-empty glass at his grandfather's elbow. "I'm surprised to see you drinking."

"It's only that fake stuff," James said morosely. "Louise would have my hide otherwise."

"Is that what happens when you're in love?"

"You get to be my age, you learn to be grateful for the small things in life. Like Viagra." The old man slapped his knee and cackled.

"Gramps, there are some things we youngsters *really* don't need to know."

James slugged back the last of his near-beer. "Who are you calling a youngster? You're nearly middle-aged."

"I'm feeling it, too, seeing everyone all lovey-dovey. Next it'll be you and Louise tying the knot."

His grandfather smiled. "Truth is, I asked her. She told me she had to think about it."

"Really?"

"Yup. Kind of the 'it's not broke, why fix it' attitude."

"How do you feel about that?"

"I'm happy either way. Makes her secure to know I'm willing to make an honest woman out of her. It still feels a bit risque, living in sin. Keeps me on my toes, knowing she could walk anytime. Maybe that's the plan."

Sloan shifted uncomfortably and changed the subject.

"What's Cassidy do for work?"

"She's a busy lady—a midwife who travels around helping women prepare for childbirth."

"You mean she delivers other people's babies?"

"I guess that, too."

"I had no idea. It seems so . . . so intimate." The thought hit him that Cassidy might be hoping to have a kid or two of her own someday. Could *that* be her secret agenda?

"Smart girl. Hard worker, too." Gramps cocked one beetle brow. "Don't trifle with her, Sloan. Gals like Cassidy aren't the trifling type."

So why was she trifling with *him*? Just for the sex, or was there more to it?

"Well, I'm off. Time for my afternoon nap." James sent Sloan a rakish wink and made his exit.

"Another beer, sir?" the bartender asked.

Sloan glanced at his watch. "No, thanks." He'd thought his half-hour wait would heighten the anticipation of being with Cassidy, not raise a ton of doubt.

He used the key she'd given him to let himself into the dark stateroom illuminated by a couple of lit candles. The air smelled spicy-sweet, of flowers and cinnamon. The room was empty.

"Cass?"

"I'm in the bathroom. Don't come in, I— Oh!"

She was traveling in style, for she had a suite with a balcony and a queen-size bed. Sloan perched on the edge of the bed. "Everything all right in there?"

Her voice was muffled. "Not really."

"Can I help?"

"I don't know."

Now what? "Well, let me know, okay?"

He heard the knob turn, then Cassidy came out wearing a slinky black mini straight out of Frederick's of Hollywood.

"The zipper got caught and—"

"Turn around. I'll fix it."

The zipper was more than caught, it was mangled into the slick fake-rubber material and it only took him a few tugs to feel the fabric shred beneath his fingers.

"I hope its under warranty," he muttered.

She turned around, half-in and half-out of the ridiculous front-laced garment. Her laugh sounded forced. "So much for my seductive-siren routine."

Something didn't feel quite right to Sloan. He slowly ran his nails the length of her bare arm and felt her shiver. "Why don't you get dressed and we'll go up to the bar and have a drink? Make sure we're both on the same page with this arrangement."

"Oh, no you don't. We had a deal."

He watched her from beneath narrowed lids. Something was definitely up, but what?

Sloan cast his eye about the stateroom and spied a bottle of champagne on ice. He rose and made short work of opening the bottle and pouring two glasses.

"Hon, I appreciate the effort you went to but it really wasn't necessary. You had me at 'hello.' "

"That's from *Jerry McGuire*," she said dismissively.

"It's also from here." He took her hand and placed it flat on his chest. "Cassidy, you must know you don't need any special props for seduction."

She appeared to be weighing his words as she took a sip of her champagne. "I wanted to be sure our time together was memorable."

A thought struck. "You're not a virgin, are you?"

"Hardly," she scoffed.

"Just had to ask," he mumbled, feeling more awkward by the second. He should've just dragged her off when the urge first struck.

Silence hung between them and he cleared his throat. "There's one other thing I need to know."

"What's that?"

"Are you on the pill?"

"Of course I am. Why?"

"I wanted to be sure your biological clock isn't ticking out of control, 'cause I don't want to have kids. Not ever."

"Really. Why's that?" she asked curiously.

"Lots of reasons."

"But . . . you haven't had a vasectomy?"

"No."

"If you feel that strongly, why expect the woman to always take care of it?"

Sloan bristled. "I use a condom."

"I would hope so." Cassidy sighed into the silence. "This is getting really heavy. It's supposed to be a fun romp, and I blew it with this stupid outfit."

"It *is* sexy, in a kinky sort of way." He moved in close.

She batted her eyes. "Do you like kinky?"

"Sure. So why don't you slither out of that getup and let's get down to business?"

He stood and pulled his T-shirt over his head from the back, then dropped it on the floor. God, he was beautiful; a symmetry of ripped muscle, the result of long hours of physical labor, rather than the gym. His chest was peppered with just the right amount of dark brown hair and she longed to bury her face there, to inhale his fragrance, his taste.

"I think this thing is stuck on," Cassidy said as she tugged at the neckline. "It's not exactly a breathable fabric."

"Have no fear. Sloan Hardt to the rescue." He pulled a pocketknife from his jeans pocket and she felt the dull edge of cold steel against her skin as he sawed at the front lacings till her breasts sprang free.

"Much better." He put the knife away and dipped his head forward for a taste. As he swept his tongue across her nipples, Cassidy's knees went weak. She held his head in place and ran her hands through his thick dark hair, noting the marked contrast against her white skin.

"You've grown up," he said, cupping her breasts in his palms, brushing them against his bare chest. "I remember when you were flat as me."

"Are you going to cut me loose from the rest of this?"

"I don't know," he teased. "It's kind of growing on me."

"But I need you now," she said in her most seductive voice.

He pulled her tight against him so her breasts brushed his hair-spangled chest, then gripped her behind and pulled her up against his hardness. Slowly he rolled up the garment's hemline so he could fondle her bare tush.

She dipped one hand down the front of his jeans, her finger brushing the velvet-soft tip of his erection. He growled in her ear as she unzipped his jeans and set him free.

"You're not wearing underwear. I like that," she murmured.

His cock was as magnificent as the rest of him, long and thick and pulsating with the desire to pleasure her. She sank to her knees before him, ran her hands lovingly across his balls and up the length of his erect cock, then tongued the tip in slow, teasing circles.

He was steely hard with a satin overlay, standing patient for her exploration as she widened the circles, her tongue making its way up and down his shaft. She ringed the base with her thumb and forefinger and pumped as she licked. Before long, he reached down and pulled her to her feet.

"Don't you like that?"

"Entirely too much." His eyes bored into hers with that intensity that had always stolen her breath as he peeled out of his jeans. She ran her hands freely up and down his chest, loving the crisp springing hair, the hard cushion of muscle, the texture of his skin.

"You feel so good." She closed her eyes to commit him to memory.

He responded in kind, running his hands up and down her arms and shoulders and back.

"Are you going to leave me trussed up like this or cut me free?" she asked.

"Hmmmm . . . I like the kinkiness of this outfit. After all, I can reach all the important parts." He cupped her rounded bottom in one hand, ran the fingers of his free hand across her Venus mound, and licked her exposed breasts.

Heat raced like wildfire through her bloodstream and she gave a sexy wiggle. "I may die of sexual frustration."

Chapter Three

He grinned. "There's my thanks for getting you off earlier."

"That was only a taste," she pouted.

He urged her down to the edge of the bed. "And I need a better taste."

She lay propped on her elbows as he cut through the rolled-up hem of her dress, then slid the blade up the front like a hot knife in butter.

Cassidy pulled it out from beneath her and tossed it across the room. She quivered in anticipation as he traced a line from her throat, between her breasts, to her navel, then tickled her hip bones.

"Tell me why you thought you needed props," he said, his hands cupping her hips and tilting her pelvis.

"I wanted to make sure you didn't still see me the way I used to be, homely and fat."

"You were cuddly-plump, with a smart mouth, and fun to be around."

"I'm even more fun now." She caught him off guard, pushed him over and straddled his middle, bracing herself with her hands on his chest. "Since the first time's never good, let's get it out of the way so we can move on."

He grabbed her upper arms. "Who told you the first time's never good?"

"It just never is."

He rolled over so she was pinned beneath him. "Sweetheart, hold on for the ride of your life."

Cassidy sighed and welcomed his kiss, which didn't stop with her lips. Inch by inch he traveled from her neck and shoulders to her breasts, then over her rib cage to her belly button, before skimming across from hip bone to hip bone.

She stretched her arms luxuriously above her and felt her body come sensuously alive, like a dormant seed slowly coaxed awake by the sun.

He licked and nibbled and kissed his way down one leg and up the other, massaging her muscles at the same time. "Roll over."

How could she refuse him anything, especially when he subjected her back to the same torturous journey of his lips and tongue? She felt the damp heat of his mouth run down her spine to her tailbone, before switching tactics to nip her buttocks.

"You have a beautiful back. And an even more beautiful ass. The softest skin." His hands were everywhere, blazing a path for his foraging mouth, shooting sparks of sensation through her bloodstream from a thousand spiraling pinpoints.

His sleek male contours found her softer female counterparts as he finally rolled her over to face him. His hands eased her legs farther apart and he gently unfolded her hidden treasures, dipped his finger into her inner sweetness, then transferred it to his mouth, savoring her special flavor. All the while, his eyes never stopped devouring every inch of her.

This was exactly the way she'd seen it play out in her mind. Sloan Hardt panting for her, taking her places she'd never been before, raw, primitive, and basic, like the man himself.

His touch teased her, little more than a whisper against her skin, a gentle rain against her inner thighs where soft, trimmed curls guarded her female nest.

She wasn't accustomed to this type of buildup and anticipation, but Sloan wasn't about to be rushed.

His eyes met hers. "What are you thinking?"

"I'm glad I made this offer."

"Me, too. I have never wanted to please a woman as much as I want to please you."

Feeling her confidence soar, she undulated beneath his touch. "I'm all yours."

He mumbled something that sounded like, "I wish," just

before he dipped down to her inner sanctum, replacing his fingers with his tongue.

He traced her inside and out as if he'd always known her: when to lick, when to probe, when to tantalize with swirls and special moves that had her rising up off the bed.

The divine buildup of pleasure rippled through her with gathering momentum, growing in intensity like a high-pitched note of music capable of shattering glass, shattering her.

When she exploded with a scream, Sloan covered her mouth with his, absorbing her aftershocks and sharing the sweetness with her.

The euphoric glow dissipated slowly, leaving Sloan looking mighty pleased with himself, as he should. She smiled at him. "Your turn."

He knelt between her thighs and she braced herself for his entry. Still he took his time, rubbed himself all over her, inside and out, sharing her moist excitement, anointing himself with her juices until she all but screamed her frustration and lifted her hips to entice him in.

He nuzzled her with his tip, then drew back with a teasing smile.

"You're killing me!"

He nudged her clit with the velvety tip, rolled it across her engorged lips, and finally, slowly inserted it, inch by torturous inch.

He pulled out, then eased back in, again and again, increasing his pace, increasing the friction, edging the tension to a point that seemed unbearable. Just as she almost crested, he stopped.

"What's wrong?" Cassidy panted, stroking his hair, his shoulders, his back, every place within reach.

"Not a thing." He rolled, taking her with him so she was on top. "Just wondering what your favorite position is." His hands on her hips encouraged her to find her best angle and speed. "How's that?"

She leaned back in a graceful arc and caught her weight on her hands behind her, then bobbed up and down a few times. "Not bad." Then she bent forward, brushing her breasts teasingly across his chest. He pulled them to his mouth, sucking greedily in a way that sent a fresh flood of heated desire to her V Zone. She rocked back and forth on him, then, mimicking his earlier actions, she pulled away and rubbed herself on his tip before slowly reinserting him.

He captured her hands and placed them on her breasts.

"Touch yourself. Everywhere it feels good."

Shyly at first, then with growing boldness, she massaged her sensitive nipples. Ripples of pleasure were compounded by the divine pressure of Sloan pulsing deep inside her, and she leaned forward, then back, then forward again to increase the pressure on her pleasure bud.

When Sloan gently thumbed the sensitive nub, she shuddered at the sudden explosion inside her. Before she'd caught her breath from her orgasm, Sloan turned her around on her knees and was inside her again, fast and furious, making her aftershocks quickly crest into new eruptions that had her panting and moaning and clutching the sheets as, with a hoarse cry, Sloan emptied himself inside her.

Cassidy slowly sank down onto her stomach, careful not

to dislodge him. She curled onto her side, enjoying the way he spooned her from behind as their breathing slowly returned to normal.

"You're right," she said when she could finally speak. "First times don't always have to be disappointing."

"Wait till you see what I do for an encore," he promised.

"I can't wait." It felt too good lying here with him in the afterglow, and she reminded herself not to get used to it.

Sloan woke with a start, Cassidy tucked against his shoulder, and glanced at the clock. Three a.m. Would she expect him to stay the night? He usually avoided that, due to the morning-after awkwardness and the fact that, in the woman's eyes at least, a shared night meant a commitment to spend the next day together. He'd always used the ranch as his excuse, but here he had none.

As he was wondering how to ease out without waking her, the stillness was shattered by a loud buzzing noise from the closet.

Cassidy stirred next to him and blinked awake. "What's that noise?"

"Sounds like an angry nest of bees." Happy for the excuse, he sprang from the bed and followed the sound to a velvet drawstring bag hanging in the closet.

"Give me that!" Cassidy pulled the bag from his hand, her face bright red as she delved inside and quieted the noise.

Sloan stood there with a grin, his arms folded across his chest. "What's in the bag, Cass?"

"It . . . nothing. It's just my vibrators."

"Wanting to join the action, were they? How many are there?"

He reached for the bag but Cassidy put it behind her back, out of reach. "I went to this sex shop and there were all these different toys and the clerk assured me men enjoy them, too, so I . . . I bought some. You know. In case."

"In case I got tired?" Sloan asked, biting back his laughter.

"In case you couldn't measure up," she said cockily.

"If you're challenging me, be prepared to accept the consequences."

Just the sight of Cassidy's soft fragrant curves, coupled with the musky smell of sex, worked its magic on his senses. He swaggered back toward the bed, his cock fully charged and ready for action.

Her lips curved into a very feminine smile as she reached for him. "And what consequences might those be?"

He stood before her and enjoyed her tentative exploration as she smoothed her small hand down his length, top first, then the underneath. She made a loose fist and ringed him. "Show me what you like."

He ran his fingers through her hair. "What you're doing feels damn fine."

She dipped her head and tongued the sensitive tip. He tightened his fingers in her hair, signaling his pleasure.

Bolder then, she took him into her mouth and tightened her fist down near the root, pumping her hand and sucking him at the same time.

"Oh God, Cass." It was the sweetest torture and he didn't want her to stop.

With her free hand she gently stroked his balls, then cupped them in her palm while her tongue did some fancy swirl action that was nearly his undoing.

"Whoa, that's almost too fine." He climbed into bed next to her, knelt between her legs, and lifted her hips up off the mattress. She took her cue from him and locked her ankles behind his back. He could feel her heat, smell her desire, glimpse the deep blush rose of her inner petals, quivering in anticipation.

"Are you ready?

She nodded.

"Make sure," he said.

He saw confusion in her eyes. "Touch yourself. Make sure you're wet enough."

She gave it a quick, tentative pass. "I'm wet."

"Show me how good it can feel."

As she trailed her fingers south to the valley of pleasure, he watched her slowly unfold like a rose to the sun. She touched herself inside and out, fingers glistening with the moisture of her desire.

"God, you're so beautiful." He lifted her hips higher and she tightened her legs behind him. "Tell me how it feels."

Her eyes were dreamy, lids languid as she slowly caressed herself. He could hear the soft whispering *shush* as she rubbed herself faster, dipping in and out of her delicate opening.

"It feels beautiful," she said. "So soft. Warm at first, now hot."

"Tell me when you're just about ready to come."

But he needed no words; he felt it—a tension that started

at her feet and radiated through her limbs. Just before she hit it, he plunged into her. It was a crazy jump-start of a ride, her bucking and writhing beneath him, rearing up into him, spiraling out of control and taking him with her.

Afterward, he went into the bathroom to wash himself, then took her a damp face cloth. He kissed her forehead.

"Where are you going?"

"Back to my cabin to grab a few hours' sleep."

She glanced toward the porthole where the sky was lightening. "It's almost dawn." She stifled a yawn.

He nodded, pulling on his jeans and shirt. "I'll see you at the wedding."

As Sloan closed the door behind him and went silently down the corridor, he wondered why he didn't feel the normal relief at having escaped.

Chapter Four

Sloan unlocked his door and flipped on the light inside his cabin.

"What the—"

His father rolled over in the second bed and swore at him.

"What the hell are you doing here?" Sloan crossed the small room and removed his watch.

"Your mother had some weird superstition about seeing each other the night before the wedding. I had the steward let me in. Wondered when you might show up."

"For the record, the sun's just coming up on your wedding day."

"Where have you been?"

"The casino."

Rake lobbed a pillow at him. "Be as chivalrous as you want, but don't lie to your old man. I was there till three."

"How'd you do?"

"Probably nowhere near as well as you."

Sloan couldn't help his smirk. "It shows, huh?"

"You've got Cassidy Ferrill written all over you."

Sloane could still taste her. "I had several years of neglect to atone for. Any words of wisdom about women for me on your wedding day?"

Rake shrugged and rolled out of bed. "You'll do what you want, like you and Steele always do." He headed into the tiny bathroom and Sloan heard the shower start up. "Besides, I'm hardly one to be handing out advice," Rake called over the sound of water.

"Ditto to that." Sloan peeled out of his clothes, set the alarm for a few hours later, and fell into bed.

After sleep and a shower, Sloan stumbled into one of the ship's restaurants, slid into an empty seat next to his grandfather and Louise, and signaled the waiter for coffee, stifling a yawn as he spooned in sugar.

"Late night?" Gramps asked with a look that saw too much.

"I didn't get much sleep."

"You youngsters," Louise said. "Cassidy was still asleep, too."

Conscious of the way James's eyes brightened, Sloan asked, "What time's the wedding again?" to deflect attention away from himself.

"It's scheduled for eleven. I'd better go start getting ready." Louise took a final sip of her tea, then left.

"Why's the wedding so early?" Sloan asked his grandfather.

"Something to do with the right light for the outdoor pictures. Or maybe it's the champagne brunch. Who really knows or cares? We menfolk go where we're told, when we're told."

"I guess." Sloan stirred his coffee, staring into its unfathomable depths.

"Might as well spit it out before things start hopping around here."

"What do you mean?"

"I always knew when something was stuck in your craw. You and Steele both."

"You did, didn't you?" He stared at the ceiling, choosing his words. "You never stayed out all night when we were kids. Never had women overnight, either. Was that because you didn't want to? Or because of us?"

James cracked a grin. "You boys were a mighty handy excuse."

"You're not answering the question."

"If you're not in a bed in the first place, there's no problems getting out afterward."

"Jeez, Gramps!" Sloan blinked away unwanted visuals. "Not on an empty stomach."

His grandfather let out a ribald laugh. "There were ladies who'd have liked me to spend the night. Didn't seem very gentlemanly to give them false hope."

Sloan nodded. "That's how I see it, too. What made Louise different?"

"Ever think maybe it's me who's different?"

"I don't see you slowing down any."

"There comes a time in every man's life when he realizes one good woman is everything he needs." He slyly nudged Sloan with his elbow. "Until then, the candy store has lots of samples."

Sloan took a sip of his coffee. "Cassidy made me a crazy offer. Her and me, for the duration of the cruise, then we walk away, no regrets."

"Sounds like you're not buying what she's selling."

"I'm not sure what to think."

"Nothing wrong with making memories. So it sounds like this is the perfect time to give you these." He passed Sloan a ring of keys.

"What's this?"

"Entry to a world behind locked doors: the reason they call it the Fantasy Cruise Line."

Sloan stared at the collection of keys, fascinated. He'd heard all about the Fantasy Cruises, where a person's fantasies knew no limits.

"Louise said I already brought her fantasies to life. And at our age, she likes me best in a soft bed."

Sloan pocketed the keys. "Sounds like I have your blessing."

Gramps rose. "What the Ferrill women want, the Ferrill women have a habit of getting. May as well enjoy the ride." He sauntered off whistling.

Sloan shook his head as he watched him leave. Did life get any weirder?

On his way back to his cabin he ran into his mother, who didn't look her usual calm and collected self. In a totally uncharacteristic move, she hurled herself into his arms with a sob.

"The wedding's off! What should I do, Sloan? How will I tell all the guests?"

"Hold it! Whoa! What's this all about?"

"Your father. I don't know where he is! He stayed out all night. He's jilting me, I just know it."

"Mom, Dad was with me last night. You told him it was bad luck to spend the night before your wedding together and he respected your wishes."

She drew back half a step. "Why didn't he tell me that?"

"He probably figured it went without saying."

"Communication always was Rake's weak point." She gave him a watery smile.

"Didn't you teach us that men and women communicate completely differently?"

Her smile widened. "You mean you were actually listening to something I said?"

"Hey, anything that gives me a leg up with the ladies."

"You never needed any help in that area."

"Since Steele was always Mr. Strong, Silent, and Aloof, I got the ladies by default. They didn't mind using me to catch his eye. Worked for me." He put an arm around his mother's shoulders. "Now, let's go find your bridesmaids. You have a wedding to get ready for."

She paused. "It's not a problem that I invited Cassidy, is it?"

"No, Mom. It's not a problem at all."

The problem was him. And the fact that Cassidy was different from other women he'd been with. Not that he was having second thoughts; he was all for having a good time. But he had the feeling that the moves he'd perfected in the past had in no way prepared him for what lay ahead. And he couldn't shake the feeling that she was up to something.

He still hadn't figured things out to his satisfaction by the time he knocked on the door to Cassidy's cabin. He had the key she'd given him, but it didn't feel right to just let himself in.

"Oh, good. Can you zip me?" She looked harried, with pin curls in the front of her hair, her face dewed with perspiration.

"No problem." He accomplished the task, letting his hands linger over the rounded curve of her ass.

She pushed his hands away. "We're already late."

"Don't worry—Angel and Rake have never been on time in their lives."

"That doesn't make my tardiness acceptable. It's all your fault I slept in."

"Maybe I can make that up to you?"

"You!" She stomped into the bathroom, yanking out hairpins as she went.

He followed her to the doorway and leaned against the frame, watching her attack her hair with a brush.

"I ran into my mom earlier. She was freaking out and ready to call off the wedding because my dad didn't go back to their cabin last night."

"What?" Cassidy whirled to face him, her mouth a disbelieving O.

"Yeah. She'd told him it was bad luck to spend the night together, then freaked because he actually listened for once."

"Is everything all right?"

"Till next time. They've been doing this so long, it's practically its own lounge act." He paused. "Last night was great, Cass. But if you've changed your mind about the rest of the cruise . . ."

She straightened, hands on hips. "Don't tell me I'm too much woman for the infamous Sloan Hardt?"

He laughed out loud. "Is that what this is about? Are you trying to prove that you can have any man you want?"

"I *can* have any man I want. This week I just happen to want you," she said.

He pulled her close and kissed her. "Lucky me."

Sloan escorted her down the aisle and deposited her in the seat next to her mother, then took his place at the front of the chapel next to Steele. This was *not* going to be as easy as she'd originally thought. Sloan was nobody's fool and she'd caught his gaze on her more than once, as if trying to see through to her true motives. She'd expected him to just take the sex without giving it a second thought, but clearly he'd changed, too.

Ever since Cassidy had morphed into a swan, she'd inspired lust in men, which was okay to a point. But now she wanted more, which was why she was practicing her wiles on Sloan. She needed to make him fall in love with her in order for her transformation to be complete.

For a moment last night, she thought he might have figured out that she wanted more than to sow her wild oats, but she was probably giving him too much credit. Since when did a man see any farther than the end of his nose?

The air was laden with the scent of fresh flowers and a ripple of anticipation ran through the waiting crowd. Cassidy looked over her shoulder to see people jammed into the back of the tiny chapel, standing room only.

"It looks like they invited the entire ship," she told her mother.

The music started and Angel proceeded down the aisle on James's arm, wearing that special glow reserved for a bride.

As she looked around at the happy couples witnessing Angel and Rake's renewed commitment to each other, Cassidy felt immense satisfaction at being here with Sloan. She'd get what she came for. Full circle.

Sloan had left pretty hastily in the wee hours. Did he not want to fall asleep next to her and waken in her arms? Maybe getting him to do that would be the true test of her power.

"Shall we?" Suddenly he was standing before her, drop-dead handsome in his black tuxedo, his arm crooked her way. "Angel insists on the photos before the reception."

"And the bride should always be indulged," she agreed.

When they joined the family on deck, Sloan pulled her toward the group being arranged by the photographer and Cassidy stopped.

"I'm not really family," she demurred.

"Close enough." He kissed her long and hard and she pulled back, slightly dazed, to the sound of applause and the click of the camera.

It wasn't easy but she turned and took a bow, aware of Sloan's approving smile. Sloan's approval made her feel warm and fuzzy, which wasn't right. She didn't need anyone's approval but her own.

The photo taking finally over, their group filtered in for the brunch, and Sloan left her side to go sit at the head table.

Cassidy sipped her champagne, fantasizing about their next romantic interlude. How long before he fell for her, crushed to find out she didn't return his feelings?

She jumped when she felt a tap on her shoulder. "Excuse me, miss. If you wouldn't mind following me." The steward at her elbow passed her a folded note. "From your gentleman friend."

Cassidy unfolded the thick vellum with the ship's logo. "Come to me, Cass." Signed with an S.

The steward led her to an elevator that required a special key, then onto a floor she hadn't been to before, a maze of hushed corridors illuminated by subdued lighting.

He stopped in front of an unmarked door, knocked once, then melted from sight.

The door swung open and Cassidy entered a darkened room. As her eyes adjusted to her surroundings, she saw that the room wasn't totally dark, although dim and cavelike. Faint strains of music in the background grew louder in welcome. It was cowboy country, a song she didn't recognize. In the distance she could see the faint glow of lights grow brighter in time to the music. She jumped as a spotlight suddenly illuminated a mechanical bull in the center of the room. She had barely taken a step toward it when she heard the soft *whoosh* of air overhead, seconds before a lasso settled around her middle, pinning her arms to her sides as she was slowly drawn forward.

Sloan stepped into the circle of light, the other end of the lasso resting in his gloved hands, his face in shadow beneath the brim of a Stetson. As he reeled her in closer she saw that he wore leather chaps, cowboy boots, and a leather vest over his bare chest, the ridges of muscle in his arms and chest clearly defined as he pulled her in.

Her heart pounded and her mouth felt suddenly dry. She licked her lips. "You seem to have me at your mercy."

"Yes, ma'am," he said with a cowboy drawl.

She quivered in anticipation as his gaze met hers, then shifted to the mechanical bull. "Are you planning to show me your prowess on that creature?"

"That's exactly what I plan to do."

The song changed to a popular love-gone-wrong country ballad, which Cassidy knew she would never listen to again without recalling this moment, the tension in the room, the tingle of excitement and anticipation thrumming through her veins as Sloan slowly circled her.

"Climb up on the bull and face me."

"You'll have to untie me first."

"All right." He slid the rope up over her torso, his gloved hands freely roaming her waist and breasts, and he slapped her on the backside as she turned to climb on. She could feel the seams of his gloved hand through the thin silk of her dress, and her bottom tingled as she perched on the sheepskin-draped saddle.

Suddenly, her hands were grabbed and taped together onto the bull behind her.

"We can't have you falling off, now can we?" Moving in front of her, Sloan placed her legs on either side of her mount. Her dress rode up, exposing a long expanse of bare legs, and she felt wickedly daring, sexy, and provocative. Her eyes lingered on his chest before following the treasure trail to where the faded denim lovingly accentuated the bulge of his arousal.

He drew one glove off with his teeth and grazed each leg from knee to thigh with the tips of his fingers. Her nipples visibly hardened with excitement as he got closer and closer to her V and she squirmed a little, encouraging him to venture closer. Her damp thong underwear was rubbing against her clit and she'd gladly trade it for Sloan's finger.

Sloan smiled as the mechanical bull began to move beneath her, a gentle, undulating sway that further aroused and stimulated her.

"Lean forward," Sloan said.

She did so, confident she wouldn't fall off because of the way he'd taped her hands.

"Oh!" She could feel subtle vibrations, as if the bull had a built-in vibrator in just the right spot.

"You like that?"

"Oh yeah."

A second vibration started just beneath her bottom and she swayed gently forward and back with the bull's motions, enjoying the stimulation to both erogenous zones.

"Highly effective," she said. "Don't you want to play?"

"I will; I want to watch you come first."

"Do I get to watch you watching me?" she said as her body rocked back and forth with the bull's movements. She tugged her confined hands, unable to free them. Her breasts ached to be touched and everything inside her tightened in anticipation as Sloan watched her.

"Your nipples are hard," he said huskily. "I can see them pressing against your dress."

"Take them in your mouth," she said. "Suck them."

"My pleasure." He dampened each silk-draped nipple with his tongue, then sucked hard through the thin fabric before teasing her with his teeth.

Her breath rose and fell in harsh pants. Sloan gave a side-to-side provocative hip swing, followed by the ripping sound of Velcro.

His getup was a stripper's costume! One easy move left him in the chaps but fully exposed, the tip of his erect penis brushing her bare thigh as he transferred his attention from her breasts to her mouth. He thrust his tongue in and out of her mouth, mimicking the sex act, and when she climaxed he swallowed her screams of pleasure, then held her close as her body shuddered in the aftermath and she struggled to catch her breath.

When the bull slowed and stopped, he climbed on and straddled her. He loosened her hands and she guided him to her, rubbing him around and around, teasing herself as much as she teased him. Finally she could stand it no more and lowered her head to taste him.

She brushed her lips up and down his engorged length, then back to the tip, which she tasted with just the end of her tongue. His erection tasted of her and she opened wider, admitted just the tip, and heard him moan.

He reached between them and teased her with his fingers.

She was melting against his fingertips, soft and swollen and open, and took another inch of him into her mouth, then swirled her tongue in zigzags. He shuddered in response, pulled free, and tugged her onto his lap. She wiggled out of her thong panties and dress and straddled him, slowly dragging herself along his length and then onto him. She moved back and forth with him just inside the entranceway.

His eyes never leaving hers, he reached up to palm her breasts. "I can hold out as long as you."

"Probably longer." She lowered herself onto him and caught her breath at the incredible rightness of him inside her.

"God, Cassidy!" He surged upward in a move that filled her completely, yet left her hungry for more.

She balanced her weight with her hands on his chest, feeling the friction of him in her, out of her, then back in. She shifted her hands to his shoulders, angling herself so there was more friction to her clitoris and G-spot.

"Make me come again," she begged.

Chapter Five

"Whatever the lady wants." He watched the dreamy haze of satisfaction suffuse her features; eyes half-closed, lips parted in a half smile of expectation and anticipation. He felt the surge of her female power surrounding him, engulfing him as her body gloved his, a perfect fit.

Her breath caught in little pants as another orgasm started to build and her movements intensified as she rode him toward the ultimate pleasure peak. He reached down to where their bodies joined, slick and damp, and found her swollen love knot. He rubbed it with his bent thumb, then bit his lip as she writhed and moaned atop him, finally surrendering with a keening cry as the internal explosion took her far beyond and away from him.

She returned to sag against him, her internal sheath pulsing with the aftermath of release. He sipped her sigh of pleasure from her lips as he held her close in the circle of his arms.

"I don't think I can move," she murmured.

He said nothing.

"Am I too heavy?" He heard shades of the former chubby teen in her voice.

"Never." He smoothed the delectable curve of her bottom, then gave her a light pinch. "I liked you with a little more weight on."

She straightened to give his chest a playful slap, then realized he was still hard.

"You didn't come yet."

"No hurry."

Careful not to dislodge their joining, he turned her in his lap so he could nibble the back of her neck. He felt a shudder of response ripple down her spine and followed it with his tongue as far as he could. Her skin was salty with perspiration and he gorged himself on the taste of her as he palmed her breasts, loving the way her nipples leapt to attention as she moaned her approval.

As he played with them, he felt a fresh flood of damp heat envelop his cock. She obviously felt it, too, for she reached down and rubbed his balls one at a time, tracing the seam before she cupped them together. All the while, he thrust in and out of her in slow deliberation. It was a whole new friction, a sensation she clearly loved as she melted and pulsed around him.

When he increased his pace, she did, as well. His hands gripped her hips, controlling the speed at which they thrust and parried until, with a hoarse cry, he surrendered all control. Cassidy looped one arm behind to hold him close with a sexy arch of her back that made her breasts jut forward, too tempting not to fondle.

"Feel better?" he asked.

"Much," she murmured. "Are there other rooms like this on the ship?"

"For any fantasy you want to play out. Hey! Where are you going?" Somehow, without him even realizing it, she had slipped from his arms and into her dress.

"I need a shower." She dropped a kiss on his forehead. "Besides, I'd prefer it if we weren't seen leaving together."

"But . . ."

Sloan watched the door close behind her. Was this the way she'd felt when he'd slipped out of bed in the wee hours? Was she doing it on purpose?

No, Cassidy wasn't like that; she probably meant exactly what she said. He was less eager to wash the scent of her from his skin, enjoying her lingering fragrance and taste as he considered what fantasy to take on next.

Eventually he forced himself to move. He missed Cassidy, he realized, as he showered and changed. And the ship was far larger than he'd thought, because he couldn't find her anyplace, or his family. Till he got to the casino.

Cassidy was at the craps table, the dice in her cupped

palms, her face flushed with excitement, Rake on one side, Steele on the other.

He made his way to his mother, who sat with Gramps and Louise. "Honeymoon over already?"

"Sloan, where have you been?"

"Checking the ship out. What did I miss?"

"Cassidy's having beginner's luck," Louise said.

"Isn't half the secret knowing when to walk away?" Sloan didn't like how close Steele stood to Cassidy, which was dumb, since Steele was crazy in love with his wife.

Angel turned to Louise. "Cassidy is so lovely. I'm surprised she's still unattached."

"I'm afraid her father and I weren't exactly a blueprint for a happy marriage," Louise said with a sigh.

"You can't blame yourself."

"Mother guilt is an easy hat to wear."

"Where's Montana?" Sloan asked, in an obvious subject change.

"She's napping." He found himself under the scrutiny of eyes that saw too much. "You look tired. You should probably do the same before dinner."

A great idea, if he could convince Cassidy to join him. Anticipation for their next fantasy sent a surge of blood to his loins. He straightened as she approached, hoping his reaction wasn't obvious to the rest of the group. Cassidy's eyes were shining as she spilled a generous handful of chips onto the table in front of them.

"The guys say to cash out while I'm ahead. What do you think, Sloan?"

"You're asking the wrong Hardt." The second he spoke, he knew his words had come out sounding more curt than he intended. She scooped up her winnings and headed for the cashier's cage.

"That wasn't very nice, Sloan," Angel said reproachfully. "She only asked what you thought."

"How the hell do I know?" He'd never felt this possessive surge toward a woman before. He watched her across the room, not even aware he was scowling till Montana joined them.

"What's the matter, Sloan? You look mad at the world."

"Dad snored all last night. Luckily, Mom's stuck with him now. What's the deal for dinner tonight?"

"The captain has invited us to dine at his table."

Sloan didn't want to share Cassidy even with his family, let alone everyone else.

"What's eating you?" Steele laid a loving hand on Montana's shoulder, but his words were addressed to Sloan.

"Can I talk to you for a sec? In private?"

"Sure thing."

Sloan led the way out of the casino and into a quiet corner of the conservatory next door. "Cassidy and I are reconnecting. Sort of."

"Why only 'sort of'?"

"It's impossible to read her. One minute she's all over me hot and heavy, next thing I know she's gone all frosty, like I'm not even there."

"Montana used to do the same thing."

"How did you handle it?"

Steele's face took on a faraway look. "I made her own up to her feelings. If a woman's not being honest with herself, she sure can't be honest with you."

"Cassidy said she just wants me for the cruise, then we part ways for good."

"Are you buying that?"

"I did at first. Now I'm not so sure."

"You have to get her to admit what she really wants. Once you know what that is, either it works for you or it doesn't. But you need to get her alone."

"That's easier said than done around this group."

"You could always kidnap her. That worked with Montana."

Sloan threw his brother a disbelieving look. "Are you kidding me?"

Steele shook his head. "One night I grabbed her up and got her away from the ranch and all its distractions."

"Hmmm, maybe we could blow off the big family dinner at the captain's table tonight."

"That would be a start."

Cassidy turned him down flat when he suggested they eschew the captain's table in favor of a romantic dinner-for-two. She showed up for dinner looking absolutely glam, with her hair piled loosely atop her head and escaped tendrils wisping around her kissable neck. Obviously the captain thought so, too, given the way he monopolized her through course after course that seemed to drag on forever.

Everyone else at their table was chatting with great animation and no one but him seemed to notice how the captain kept touching Cassidy as they spoke. At one point she threw back her head and laughed at something she must have found particularly witty, then rocked forward to rest one hand on the captain's shoulder, her face inches from his.

Sloan dropped his fork with a loud clatter against his plate, but no one noticed. They were all laughing and talking among themselves and he knew he had to get out of there before he lost it and embarrassed not only himself, but his entire family.

"Excuse me," he said to no one in particular as he rose and left the table.

Heading outside, he stood and stared into the inky darkness where the sky met the water. He'd never let a woman get to him like this before and he didn't like it.

He decided to blow off some steam in the adults-only pool to figure out what game Cassidy was playing. She'd gotten right into the spirit of things in the Cowboy Fantasy suite, yet at dinner, flirting with the captain, it was like their little romp had never happened.

Maybe that was it. He was used to calling the shots, having the woman hang around waiting for him to decide where and when. Now the tables were turned, with Cassidy in control, while he wanted her with him all the time, not flirting with the captain at dinner.

He changed and hit the deserted pool, swimming laps. As he neared one end of the pool, he felt his foot brush something human. He stopped midstroke, popped his head to the surface, and there was Cassidy, a water nymph.

She laughed and sent a spray of water his way, like she

knew she was making him crazy and loving every second. He grabbed her and rubbed his face in the sweet crook between her neck and shoulder, absorbing her scent and feel. She was soft and warm against him as she slid her arms around him and raised her face for his kiss.

"The captain get called to duty?" He hoped he didn't sound as jealous as he felt.

"Apparently he has a ship to see to."

"Too bad."

"Not really. He likes it."

"What do *you* like?"

She stood on tiptoes before him, her hands resting lightly on his shoulders. "I like being all alone with you in the pool at night, with the stars overhead."

He glanced skyward. "Reminds me of the ranch. Big sky, lots of stars."

"Does it remind you of anything else?"

He knew what she was getting at. "Prom night." They'd gone skinny-dipping in the river, the stars overhead their only witness. "I was a prick that night. A selfish, immature bastard."

"You were," Cassidy agreed. He could feel her body heat burning into him, the same way it had so many years ago. He would have taken her virginity that night and not given it a second thought, fool that he was. Thank God she'd stopped him when she did.

"Am I forgiven?"

"Not yet. Not quite."

"How can I make it up to you?"

"Let me see. . . ." She touched her finger to her lower lip, considering.

"Come on, Cass. If you want me to apologize on bended knee, just say so."

"Why on earth would I let you off that easy?"

"You want me to suffer, is that it?"

Cassidy smiled. She wanted him as devastated as she'd been that night, a night it had taken her a long time to move past.

"Did you ever really want something, only to have it elude you?"

He shook his head.

"That's what I thought." She turned from him and swam a few strokes before he caught her, pulling her to her feet in the chest-high water. His fingers slid beneath the side ties of her bikini bottom and she shivered at the branding heat of his touch, matched by the wanting heat in his eyes.

"I want you."

It was a start, but she wanted more. A whole lot more.

She molded her palms to his chest, feeling the wall of ridged muscle. "So what's stopping you?"

She freed her breasts from her bikini top and nuzzled his chest. Her nipples hardened against his, stimulated by the crisp curl of chest hair.

He laved the supersensitive curve where her shoulder met her neck with his tongue and she felt an outpouring of sweet heat at the juncture of her thighs. She reached for him, found his thickening length beneath his swim trunks, and heard his guttural groan of response.

His kiss was hard, hot, and hungry and she basked in the heady pleasure. *This* was the female power she had craved. The ability to turn a man to putty in her hands. And not just any man, but Sloan Hardt.

Their tongues fought a duel as she slid her hands inside his trunks, moaning approvingly at the treasure she unearthed.

"You can't be serious!" Sloan said. "Not here!"

"Why not?"

She untied one side of her skimpy bikini bottom and wrapped her legs around his waist so he was within striking distance.

Holding her clasped against him, he walked them to the corner of the pool. She felt concrete against the small of her back as Sloan cupped her bottom in his hands and angled her hips to meet his thrust.

He filled her completely, the sensation so perfect she caught her breath and held on.

She reached to where they joined, touching herself and him at the same time, the steel-hard root of his cock as it slid in and out of her soft folds. Water sloshed and rippled around them as he increased the speed and angle of his penetration. She felt her clit swell as she brushed it with her fingertip, signaling the beginning buildup of release.

Every muscle in her body tensed as her orgasm swept through her, and she collapsed against him.

"Damn," Sloan swore.

"What is it?"

"It seems we're no longer alone."

* * *

It hadn't been easy to make an unobtrusive retreat from the pool, but they'd managed it without the newcomers realizing what they'd interrupted. Cassidy bade him good night sweetly at her door and he left it at that. They had the whole trip together, after all.

The next day it had been surprisingly simple to dog Cassidy's movements and learn she had booked a private late-afternoon hair appointment. From there it was easy to convince the male hairdresser, who enthusiastically embraced Sloan's romantic fantasy, to cooperate.

Which is how Sloan came to be waiting behind the heavy burgundy velvet drapes in the posh salon till Cassidy's shampoo and scalp massage were well under way. Then, at an agreed-upon signal, he stepped in and took over. The hairdresser left, locking the salon behind him, pausing briefly to give Sloan the thumbs-up.

Sloan plunged his hands into Cassidy's sudsy hair as she reclined in the luxury-styled retro barber chair angled toward the sink, eyes shut, a blissful expression on her face. He stood behind her so even if she opened her eyes she wouldn't see him as he massaged her scalp.

She gave a little wiggle and slid deeper in her seat. "That feels wonderful. It's such a treat to have someone else wash your hair."

Subtly he ran his fingers behind her ears, then in front, tracing their shape, caressing the lobes before tunneling his hands into her hair at the crown and raking his nails down toward her brow, then back up. Gently he massaged in teasing circles, beginning with the nape, working out, then down, unable to resist adding her neck into the repertoire. She had twin knots of tension at the base of her skull and his shampoo-slippery fingers worked their magic.

Cassidy exhaled breathily, a sound that was nearly his undoing as she rocked her shoulders from side to side. "You have a great touch. You could easily have a second career doing massage."

He turned on the water before he spoke, hoping it would disguise his voice. "I like this."

"Me, too."

He tested the water against his hand to make sure it wasn't too hot. Then he lightly sprayed her hair, separating the thick wet strands and watching the rainbow of bubbles dissipate. He watched the rise and fall of her chest as she breathed, determining that she was braless beneath the tight tank top. He let the back of his hand brush her cheek, chasing imaginary bubbles, smoothing her hair back from her forehead.

He left the water running as he continued to pretend he was rinsing her hair. His hand strayed lower as he moved from the back of her neck to her shoulder blades, then forward to caress her shoulders and collarbone.

Surprised, she opened her eyes and sat up. "What are you—?" Too late, he realized she could see him in the mirrors opposite. "Where's Jon?"

"He stepped out. I stepped in."

Before he had time to think, she twisted around in her seat, grabbed the hose, and turned it on him.

"Hey!" he yelped.

Cassidy laughed. "That'll teach you."

"Two can play at this game." He grappled with her, wresting control of the hose but not before they had both been sprayed. Her tank clung to her chest, outlining the enticing shape of her breasts. As if on cue, the CD shuffle changed over to "I'm Gonna Wash That Man Right Outta My Hair" by Ella Fitzgerald.

"A timely tune." She grabbed a towel and ineffectually blotted the front of her shirt before she applied the towel to her hair, leaving it a damp tousle.

"Maybe I should investigate a new career." He stepped on the foot controls for the chair and she sank back with a shriek as her feet and legs were elevated in the air. "After all, you told me I'm good at this massage stuff."

"Prove it," she said in husky tones.

It was all the invitation he required. He pulled off her sandals and cradled one elegant bare foot in his hands. "Did you know there are seventeen thousand nerve endings in each foot?" He grazed the arch with his thumbnail as he spoke. When she gave an enticing little shudder he continued slowly rubbing and massaging her foot from heel to toes, savoring the way her entire body shivered in response, her reflection visible from a dozen different angles.

"I can't tell you how relieved I am to know it's you who was washing my hair."

"Really. Why's that?"

"I found myself getting turned on, and I was starting to drift into this fantasy. Nothing I could act out with a gay hairdresser, unfortunately."

"I wanted to apologize for being a jerk earlier."

"Which time?"

"Ouch!" He winced. "I guess I deserve that. And about making it up to you?" He slid his hands from her foot up her leg to the inside of her knee.

"Did you have something in mind?"

Sloan rose and turned out the overhead lights, leaving only the illumination from half a dozen aromatherapy candles whose faint illumination danced on the cream-colored walls, enhanced by the mirrors. She watched, eyes wide, as he picked up a towel and tore it into strips.

"Do you trust me, Cass?"

She nodded, eyes never leaving his as he made his way back to her.

He swung the armrests out so they were at a ninety-degree angle to the chair. He tied her wrists to the armrests, loosely enough that she could pull out if she wanted to. He didn't want to scare her.

"So you were getting turned on, were you?" He trailed his fingers along the soft, smooth flesh under her arm and her nipples tightened beneath the damp tank top. He continued across her collarbone, before dipping beneath the neckline of her top, enjoying the generous swell of her breasts.

Her breath caught and she licked her lips with the tip of her tongue. Slowly he lowered his head near hers, watched her lips part in anticipation before he changed his mind, turning his attention back to her feet.

He found a pump bottle of body lotion close by. Beginning with her feet, he sleeked the lotion up her legs, massaging the tight muscles and soft, firm skin, stopping just shy of the hem of her short denim skirt.

A thin strip of bare midriff between its waistband and her tank egged him on. He traced a line from hip to hip, ringed her navel, his fingers roaming relentlessly up toward her breasts.

"Sloan . . ."

"Ssshhh . . ."

He bent over her, lips and tongue following the pathway forged by his fingertips. Enjoying the taut skin of her belly as he nibbled and licked his way up to her breasts, he finally sucked each eagerly crested nipple through the thin, damp fabric.

He eased on top of her, appreciating the way the curves and contours of her body fit his. Her mouth was sweetly open, eager, ready for him, as hot and hungry as he was. He rolled his pelvis against hers to let her feel his erection, rewarded by the way she moaned deep in the back of her throat through their kiss, her pelvis arching, heightening the pressure.

He pushed her top up and exposed her breasts, which he plundered with needy hunger, rolling the nipples between his lips and tongue before giving the softest of tiny nips with his teeth. She moaned and thrashed beneath him, pulling at her bonds as she tried to get even closer.

He thwarted her again to slide down her length, hooking his thumbs beneath the waist of her skirt and panties, taking them with him.

He pushed her legs apart and admired the womanly triangle guarding the delectable pink softness of her inner chamber.

Kneeling between her legs, he raised one foot and nibbled slowly up the inside of her leg, past her knee to the soft skin of her inner thigh.

She trembled in anticipation as her breath rose and fell in tiny pants, opening fully for him, soft and pliable, trembling with need.

He traced an invisible pathway from between her breasts, over her ribs and belly to her Venus mound, before she clamped her legs around his hand.

He shook his head. "Don't make me tie your legs up." After a brief hesitation, she slowly parted her legs. He rubbed her soft inner petals and felt instant moisture against his fingers.

"Tsk, tsk. You're all wet. Perhaps we should dry you off." He turned the hair dryer on low, angling the warm air at her damp breasts, then at the treasure trove below.

He continued to fondle her with one hand and angle the warm air against her with the other. She moved beneath him, seeking release, sexy little thrusts and wiggles that were nearly his undoing. He placed two fingers at her opening, tantalizing her with their nearness. She pulled at her bonds, wiggling closer till his fingers were inside. He didn't move a muscle but let her do the work as she rode his hand, thrusting against him, hot and wet.

He abandoned the hair dryer, feeling her inner muscles clench around him, till he withdrew his hand, leaving her clit pulsing in disappointment.

He honed in for a taste and her moan of ecstasy echoed clear through him.

Gently he traced the soft shape of her arousal and the pulsing clit, quivering outer lips, flushed inner lips, and yearning opening. He dipped his tongue inside and felt her convulse beneath him.

He continued through the aftershocks and rebuilt the tides of desire until a second tremor ripped through her, followed by a third.

Her moans became a shriek, then an invitation, then a desperate plea for him.

He unfastened his jeans and knelt between her legs, lifted them up to his shoulders, and made the plunge.

He heard her cries of pleasure and delight, echoed in the way her body welcomed his.

At this angle he could see the action straight on, along with the mirrored reflection as his cock plunged in and out slowly, then fast, then slowly again despite her straining to take control, shimmying her hips from side to side, increasing the friction of their joining.

He scooped her bottom up to plunge even deeper. Her deep moan of satisfaction was followed by the internal shudders that signaled her coming orgasm. He bit hard on his lower lip and held on tight, waiting for her to break, timing his release to hers. Together they hit the heavens, then slowly drifted back to earth.

He lay atop her, listening to the frantic staccato of her heartbeat. He realized she'd worked her hands free when he felt her fingers sift through his hair.

Moments later she slipped out from beneath him and into her skirt, straightening her top. "My hair is going to be a mess at dinner tonight," she said, then sighed.

Taking his cue from her, he stood and fastened his jeans. "Just one more thing I'll need to make up to you."

Chapter Six

Cassidy took one last look in the full-length mirror. Funny, she didn't look any different. You'd think her recent shenanigans with Sloan in the beauty parlor would have left some sort of indelible mark on her. Maybe she had a split personality, Cassidy with Sloan versus Cassidy on her own.

She sighed. She'd hoped this time with Sloan would bring satisfaction, the full circle of her transformation from the girl the boys made fun of to the girl every boy lusted after. Instead, being with Sloan only seemed to muddy things, and she was still no closer to a decision about Tony. Patiently-waiting-and-eager-to-marry-her Tony; it wasn't fair to keep him waiting.

When she stepped into the hallway, she ran straight into Sloan.

He stepped back a pace, gazed up and down her body, and let out an admiring whistle. "You look hot."

"I do, don't I?" She smoothed a hand across her waist and hips. "It's funny how some days I'm still surprised when I look in the mirror, half expecting to see my former, chubby image. You probably don't know this, but Janine dumped me as her best friend after I lost weight."

"I thought girls only dumped guys."

"She couldn't handle the way men looked at me, since she was used to getting all the attention."

He nodded at the memory. "Janine always did need a lot of attention."

"And she got it. Ironic, isn't it? She sent me to the prom to keep an eye on you and keep the other girls away, then you hit on me by default."

"Hey! You told me you'd never been kissed. I took it as a wrong to right."

"We did more than kiss," Cassidy reminded him.

"I was a typical hormone-crazed boy. Can I help it if I was used to doing as much as the girl let me? I didn't expect you to feel all guilty and blab to Janine."

"Best friends don't keep those kinds of secrets from each other."

"And all this time I figured you got Janine to dump me because you wanted me for yourself."

Cassidy flushed in spite of herself. "Hardly. Who wants a two-timing boyfriend?"

"Tell me this isn't payback time."

"Don't be silly. I'm having one last fling before I get married."

"Married?" he yelped.

"That's right," she said, hoping her gamble would pay off. Men always hankered after what they couldn't have. If he knew she was spoken for, it should make him want her all the more. "Where are we going?" She hadn't been paying attention, and suddenly realized they should have reached the dining room by now.

"A shortcut," Sloan said, tightening his hold. "Why didn't you tell me you're engaged?"

"It's not official. This way doesn't seem shorter to me."

"There's something I want to show you just up ahead."

Suddenly she had déjà vu. The subdued lighting. The silent hush. The unmarked doors. "Another one of the ship's fantasy suites?"

"Good guess." Sloan unlocked a door and ushered her inside. As the door shut, they started to move.

At least it felt like they were moving. Cassidy caught her breath at the sensation of ascending in an elevator. Outside the window, the ground seemed to fall away from them on a crazy, dizzying angle and speed. It was impossible to tear her gaze away.

She pointed. "That looks like the Arc de Triomphe. Are we in Paris?"

"We are."

"And going up the Eiffel Tower. How exciting!" Cassidy pressed her nose to the glass. She'd heard about the elevator to the top of the Eiffel Tower, a sight to behold at any time but especially at night, illuminated by hundreds upon hundreds of lights; a stunning and spectacular fairyland.

Their ascent slowed to a stop and the doors slid silently open. With Sloan at her side, Cassidy moved forward to see the Paris skyline surrounding her on all sides. "So this is what it looks like from the top of the Eiffel Tower."

"Nifty, huh?"

"This can't possibly be the world-famous restaurant, can it?" For directly ahead stood an intimate bistro table set with candles and flowers, champagne chilling in a silver ice bucket.

"Even better, we're one floor above the restaurant. I took a chance and ordered dinner."

Cassidy turned to him, amazed. "Why do I have no idea what I really want until you show me?"

Sloan blew out a relieved breath in a way she found totally endearing, and she moved forward and wrapped her arms around his shoulders. "You weren't sure what my reaction would be?"

His hands settled comfortably on the curve of her waist. "You haven't exactly been predictable."

"Predictability is dull, which is why I love what you did. This was always a fantasy of mine: being whisked away for a romantic dinner where I don't even look at a menu."

"Then clearly, tonight is for you."

She curled her fingers around the lapels of his dinner

jacket and tilted her face up to his. "How do you seem to know me better than I know myself?"

He covered her hands with his. "Lucky guess?"

She reminded herself Sloan was used to having women fall in his lap. This entire trip was probably nothing out of the ordinary for him. "Is that champagne I spy?"

"Absolutely." He released her and moved to open the bottle.

It was nice to have a man take care of things. Not all the time, but what a treat to simply go with the flow and enjoy Sloan's surprise.

"The closest I've been to the Eiffel Tower is when I was in Las Vegas," she said.

"Same here." Sloan slipped a champagne flute into her hand. "And we even have romantic music." As he spoke, a jazz trio hologram appeared in the distance and "Let's Fall in Love" wafted through the simulated night air.

They stood in companionable silence, sipping champagne, enjoying the serenade.

Cassidy felt so comfortable, so easy with Sloan, yet she was intimately aware of him. The way he carried himself, his confident air, the husky timbre of his voice. Not to mention his eyes on her, promising further intimate delights.

Prickles of warmth ran up the backs of her legs to suffuse her with damp heat. Had she ever been so aware of herself as a woman? She felt as if her dormant sexuality had been brought to life by Sloan and she would never be the same.

He broke their silent bubble. "Any special plans for your big casino win? A shopping spree when we hit shore?"

"No shopping." She considered sharing her dream with

Sloan, her goal to create a drop-in house for young mothers with their babies, then decided she didn't want reality to intrude into the fantasy of their evening. "Tell me about Black Creek."

"At first I wasn't sure it was the right thing to do, leaving Gramps to fend for himself on the ranch, but it turned out to be the best thing I could have done. For everyone."

"Mom never would have moved in if you still lived there."

"Exactly. And the long-term potential for Black Creek Ranch is enormous." As he told her about the house he was building for himself, and his plans to turn Black Creek into the most productive working/dude ranch in the state, his enthusiasm was contagious.

When he mentioned that even though Steele lived on the ranch with Montana, Steele's work took him away for stretches of time, she realized that Steele had nothing to do with Sloan's running of the ranch.

She cocked her head consideringly. "Growing up, you were always a bit in Steele's shadow, weren't you?"

"Nonsense."

"I don't think so. I didn't get it back then; being an only child, I just wished I had an older sibling the way you did. But with Steele only a year older, it couldn't have been easy."

"Are you implying I'm not as good as my brother?"

She touched his arm, felt the tension of flexed muscles beneath his jacket. "Not at all. You're every bit as much of a force to be reckoned with. You've made your mark in a different way, but you're probably more like him than you'd admit."

"Ha—I'm way more subtle than him."

She laughed at that. "None of you Hardts even knows the meaning of the word 'subtle.' "

She laid her head on his shoulder, enjoying the way his arm circled her shoulder as he snugged her against him. He held her in a way that made her feel she could stay like this forever.

She shifted restlessly and edged away, wondering if she only imagined the reluctance with which he released her.

"Cass?"

"It's not a good idea—me leaning on anyone."

"You always were an independent little cuss."

"I was afraid of turning into my mother."

He laughed. "That's like me saying if I started hanging at the casinos I'd turn into Rake."

"And would you?"

"Hell no. We're all happy doing our own thing."

"And you're always there for each other. That's what family means."

He was silent for a moment. "The kind of family you never had."

"The kind I want and mean to have, assuming things work out."

"With the guy back home," Sloan said flatly. "Does he know you're here to sow a few wild oats before you settle down?"

"I learned a long time ago not to kiss and tell. Besides, he told me to take my time, to be sure."

"He's an idiot. If you were mine, I wouldn't let you out of

my sight." The intensity of Sloan's words sent a shiver through her. Would she ever inspire that sort of passion? Yes! That's why she was here.

"I don't remember you as being such a caveman," she teased. "Or maybe you just didn't care about all those girls back in high school."

He flashed a cocky grin. "It's the Hardt curse. Babe magnets, every one of us."

"That part I do remember. The Hardts breaking hearts."

"Speaking of breaking hearts, are you planning to keep the back-home prospect on the hook for long?"

"It's not that simple, Sloan."

"Sure it is. You either love the guy and want to spend the rest of your life with him, or you don't."

"He's a really nice man."

"That's a pretty lukewarm response."

"I know." She sighed. But Tony wanted the type of family she'd always longed for.

"If I was in love with a woman, I'd pursue her to the ends of the earth."

"You used to fall in love every week and I never once saw you do the pursuing."

"That's because I didn't have to," he said cheekily, just before he pulled her to him and ravished her mouth with his. There was a deep, possessive hunger in that kiss, a need she'd never equated with Sloan, and it touched her heart the way nothing else could.

He plowed his fingers through her hair, tilted her face up, and broke the kiss to stare deep into her eyes, looking for something. Some reassurance only she could give? She stared back into eyes that were blue-black with emotion, like midnight sky rimmed with thick dark lashes.

She wound her arms around his neck and felt the jump of his heart and hers, or the two of them in tandem. She sighed deeply as he kissed her again, gentler this time, but the unmistakable air of possession was a heady aphrodisiac. She was getting to him. She smelled triumph! By the end of the cruise he'd want her forever, and she'd say ta-ta.

Abruptly his embrace changed, softened into that of a dance partner as he caught her hand in his and guided her into a waltz step, keeping time to the music.

"How perfect," she murmured against his neck, inhaling the unique fragrance of his skin, soap, and aftershave.

Sloan smoothed his hands over the contours of her hips and bottom, pressing her pelvis against his. When she let out a breathy moan of pleasure and responded with a subtle pressure of her own, he gathered her closer, wanting to rip off her clothes and lose himself in her.

The thought stopped him cold. He never lost himself with a woman. He never lost the comfortable distance he maintained in an intimate relationship.

When the hell had that changed?

She'd caught him totally off guard with news of a suitor back home. The other man didn't sound like much of a threat; still, he was offering Cassidy something Sloan couldn't: a family. And it wasn't fair to deprive her of that.

He fought down the blinding jealousy that burned through him, battling the urge to brand her as his, to ensure she never forgot him as he spoiled her for all other men who followed.

Selfish!

"Are you sure you won't tell him about us?"

"Who?"

"Mr. Patiently Waiting Back Home."

"His name is Tony. And don't be absurd. Of course not."

"You two aren't even married and you're keeping secrets."

She lowered her gaze. "Everyone has secrets."

"Oh? What secrets are you hiding from me?"

"Well, I do have a secret aspiration." She peeked up at him through her lashes.

"Making love on top of the Eiffel Tower?"

"Exactly. Any way you might help me achieve that particular goal?"

"I'll see what I can do."

They were interrupted by the chime of the doorbell and Sloan reluctantly released her. "That'll be our meal. Why don't you have a seat and enjoy the view?"

Two white-jacketed waiters wheeled in meal carts and Sloan tipped them and sent them on their way.

Cassidy lifted the intriguing silver domes. "What's on the menu?"

"Escargot, to start."

When Cassidy made a face, he grinned. "Have I introduced you to anything on this trip so far that you haven't loved?" The question was delivered with a boy-devil grin, her childhood pal grown up drop-dead sexy in a way that made her melt.

She sashayed toward him, a deliberately provocative sway to her hips. "This trip is far from over."

"Touché." With one arm around her waist, he dug an escargot from its shell with a practiced motion and tucked it between her lips. When she tried to suck it from his fingertips he held fast, making her work for it before he finally surrendered the morsel. He outlined the bow of her top lip with butter-slippery fingers as she rolled it around in her mouth, exploring the taste and texture. Rich and garlicky, a tiny bit chewy.

"Not bad," she said.

He helped himself to one, then nodded. He broke off a piece of baguette and dipped it in the melted butter sauce before he offered it to her. She bit off a chunk, enjoying the contrast of crunchy crust, soft insides, and rich sauce.

"Mmmmmm." She licked her lips. "What are you going to feed me next?"

He raised a lid with a flourish. "Oysters."

She peered onto the plate. "Ugh. They forgot to cook them."

"They didn't forget." He picked up a half shell, splashed on a few drops of vodka, a pinch of horseradish, and a squeeze of lemon, then slipped it into his mouth. "Mmm. Delicious! Your turn now."

She shook her head. "I like my seafood cooked."

"You have to try at least one. They're a natural aphrodisiac."

"And you're worried I won't keep up, is that it?"

He gave her a cheeky grin. "Well, I do have plans that require all your stamina. Come on, Cass," he said coaxingly. "Here's a little one."

She eyed it with suspicion. "Do I have to chew it?"

"Do whatever feels right." He loosened the oyster with the tip of his finger and raised the half shell to her lips, pulling it away when she plugged her nose.

"Fine." He made as if to eat it himself.

She tugged on his arm. "I was kidding."

Eyes on hers, he sucked the oyster from its shell to his lips, then leaned over and passed it to her, mouth to mouth. He grinned as she chewed and swallowed. "Now that's the way to eat oysters."

"I believe it's an acquired taste," she said as she helped herself to a second one, which she doctored with a few drops of hot sauce.

"What do you think you're doing now?" Sloan asked as she reached for a third one.

"I figured I'd better seize every opportunity to outdo you in the libido department." She threw back her head and downed the oyster like a shot of tequila.

"Next time I'll order a dozen," he promised.

"At least," Cassidy said, laughing.

"I thought we'd cleanse our palates with sorbet before the next course."

"You had fun planning all this, didn't you? Do you like to cook, as well?"

"The Hardts have a motto. If you can't do it well, don't do it. I've been banned from kitchen duty for years."

"It's never too late to learn."

"Maybe if I had the right teacher—"

She danced away from him at that. His words were too intimate, hinting at a future that would never be theirs.

It was easy to get caught up in the moment, to really feel she was in Paris, dining atop the Eiffel Tower with all of Paris at her feet. She could see the tiny riverboats snaking up the Seine, lights twinkling on their decks, with passengers happily dining and dancing.

It was almost as easy to imagine that this intimacy would continue once the ship docked, which wasn't part of her master plan at all.

Sloan approached her so silently that she jumped when he touched her arm. What had happened to her internal radar, warning her when he was near?

"If madam would be so kind, the next course is served."

He had a towel over his arm, the kind old-fashioned waiters used. He escorted her to the table, pulled out her chair to seat her, then took his place across the table.

"Passion fruit sorbet," he said. "It seemed appropriate."

"Something smells delicious. What is it?"

"That's our next course: lobster. Accompanied by stuffed artichokes and crab-stuffed mushroom caps."

The sorbet was icy cold in her mouth, with a pleasant tang. She chased it with a mouthful of champagne. Divine decadence.

She put down her spoon with a clatter. Who was she trying to kid? She didn't belong here, living out her fantasy with the man of her dreams. He made her forget about her goals, and that was bad.

"What's the matter?"

She forced a smile. "No matter how fabulous, how real the dream, I know I'm going to wake up eventually."

"You were that way when we were kids, too."

"Old habits die hard."

Sloan whisked her empty sorbet dish away, refilled her champagne, and delivered the next plate with a flourish. She jumped when she felt the brush of his fingers lifting her hair, exposing her nape, then relaxed as he tied a lobster bib around her neck, all fingers and thumbs, touching and stroking the sensitive nerve endings. Shivers of delight spread up and down her spine and branched into far more intimate hollows.

"Let's see what we can do about creating new habits."

"What are you doing?"

"Cracking your lobster for you."

"No, you don't; cracking it is half the fun. I'll need a quick lesson on the artichoke, though. It looks like a thistle."

"It tastes better than it looks." He tugged off an outer leaf, dipped it in melted lemon butter, and held it up. "Don't try to eat the entire leaf. Catch it between your teeth and scrape the good stuff off, like so"—he demonstrated—"then discard the spiny center."

"A girl could starve to death, having dinner with you. Just tug off a leaf like this?"

"They get more tender as you get closer to the core. The tender, meaty inside is called the heart, and I'll show you how to eat it."

"That's the thistly part."

"Only because it's protecting the most delicate and tasty morsel."

He could have been talking about her.

"You planned this meal deliberately, didn't you? Metaphorically stripping away protective outer shells to get to the heart of things."

He laughed. "You give me far too much credit, Cass. I just chose some of my favorite foods that make eating an adventure." He cracked open a lobster claw, dug out the meat, dipped it in butter, and extended it to her. She didn't hesitate to open her mouth and let him pop it in.

They chatted as they tackled their lobsters, until abruptly the lights of Paris, including the tower and the riverboats, blinked and went out. The only illumination came from the candles on their table.

"Power outage in Paris?" Cassidy asked.

"Probably a glitch. Give it a minute."

It was a long freaky minute before there was a rumble, a shudder, and then King Kong appeared, his huge, hairy paw reaching for Cassidy.

Chapter Seven

She felt the beast's hot breath close on her skin. Clinging to the side of the tower with a front paw, he let loose with an earsplitting roar while Cassidy stared in fascination. She knew he wasn't real, yet as those dark, subhuman eyes met hers, her heart skipped in fear. Her fingers tightened on the edge of the table as all her instincts screamed *run*!

Kong gave another mighty roar and hammered the side of the tower. The table shook and dishes rattled as the swaying movement intensified and Cassidy clung to the edge of her seat.

"Sloan!" When the candles flickered and went out, Cassidy leapt to her feet as fight or flight kicked in.

Sloan rose and stood protectively between her and the beast. Kong leaned in and stared at her, so close she could feel his breath. Instinctively she edged closer to Sloan, who snugged his arm protectively around her.

"He's not real," he said reassuringly.

Still, she buried her face against Sloan's neck as Kong continued his antics. He felt good and solid and safe.

Suddenly the ground beneath them fell away. Up they rose in Kong's huge palm, eye level with the beast. Cassidy felt herself shaking from head to toe. "Oh, Lord. Tell me again that this isn't real."

"Come on." He gripped her hand hard.

"Where are we going?"

"Making a jump to safety."

"Sloan!"

"Trust me. Courage from within."

"Okay." She took a deep breath and plunged forward with him. And it really did feel like they were falling, down, down, down. "Are you sure we're not Alice falling down the rabbit hole?"

"Hang on, Cass. I won't let you down."

Their simulated fall ended with a jolt hard enough to jar the breath from her lungs.

Gradually the dark lifted and the sun rose to reveal that they were in a simulated rainfall in a beautiful tropical rain forest. The air was thick with moisture and the scent of tropical flowers, a setting so real Cassidy was surprised to find that her clothes and hair weren't wet.

She looked around. "The Garden of Eden?"

"Our own special paradise. Any place you and I are together."

She glanced away in sudden confusion, reminding herself to keep her guard up. Sloan was a master at making a woman feel special. She wasn't about to fall for that; this time it was his turn to fall!

Pretending to snuggle up to him, she picked his pocket, claiming the fantasy suites keys. "My turn to choose a key, and we'll see which door it opens. Ready?"

"Are you sure? What if it's not one of your fantasies?"

"I think I can handle it." Excitement fluttered through her as she closed her eyes, thumbed through the keys, and picked one.

He took it from her. "Let's go."

At first she was disappointed to find her key unlocked a small and intimately lit piano bar, punctuated with low-slung, comfy couches and chairs. "Can I try again?" She had hoped for something darker and more edgy, more in keeping with her mood.

"I like this." The bar's focal point, a baby grand piano, drew Sloan forward.

"Since our earlier serenade was interrupted . . ." Sloan sat down and started to play "Piano Man." Who *was* Sloan Hardt? Just when she thought she knew him, he shape-shifted into someone else entirely.

"I take requests," he invited.

"I never knew you played."

"My weekly date with Miss Gertrude, my ample-bosomed piano teacher with the mustache, was a well-kept secret in my youth."

"You mean you weren't always doing chores after school?"

"Practice was a chore, but I learned to love it."

She slid onto the piano bench next to him and watched the skilled glide of his hands across the keys. The same skilled glide with which his hands touched her, knowing which notes to play when, knowing before she did the song she sang in her heart.

It seemed the most natural thing in the world for his hands to migrate from the keyboard to her. The soft fall of his fingertips explored her bare skin, playing her arms, her neck, her shoulders and back.

He slid the spaghetti straps of her dress down her arms and unzipped her dress before she even knew he'd touched it. He picked her up and set her atop the piano's shiny surface, her thin gown a propellant as he raised her legs to rest one on either side of his waist and tugged her toward him.

The thigh-high slits on her dress gave her the freedom to follow his wishes, exposing a long line of stocking-clad legs and killer stilettos, ankle-tied with satin ribbons.

He ran his hands up her legs, then froze when he reached the top of her stockings and his fingers hit warm, bare flesh.

He gave a breathtakingly sexy smile. "I like it."

"So not all my purchases at that sex boutique were wasted?"

His fingers continued their glide, his grin widening when he confirmed that she wore a garter belt and no panties. "I'd have to say no."

He moved in for a kiss, a kiss she was dying to receive. She shrugged free of her dress straps to twine her arms around his neck. She couldn't bear not to touch him, to pull as close as possible, ankles locked behind him.

Their mouths fused in a leisurely fashion, shifting this way and that, trying each angle, seeking the perfect fit as their tongues coaxed and mated.

As his hands smoothed the line of her exposed back, sparks of awareness ignited and suffused her limbs with heat.

She felt the bodice of her dress pool at her waist, leaving her breasts delightfully stimulated by the texture of his dinner jacket.

He sucked her bottom lip into his mouth and teased it with gentle nips. She rubbed herself against him, increasing the friction to her breasts, sending lightning to her heated inner core.

She reached under his shirt to feel the soft downy hair that angled from his chest down to his navel, then tucked her fingers inside his waistband.

He broke the kiss to pull off his tie. Before she had a chance to dive for the buttons of his shirt, he positioned the tie across her eyes, knotting it behind her head. "If you can't see, you'll find all your other senses heightened."

When he moved away she felt instantly cold and alone, her perch precarious without him there. "Sloan?"

"I'm right here."

She leaned back, resting on her hands behind her for balance. She felt the returning warmth of his presence a half breath before she felt him brush against her legs, then insinuate his way between them.

He tilted her head up and she jumped as something cold

and wet hit her lips and slowly slid over her chin, down her neck, and between her breasts.

She held her breath, then forced herself to breathe as he touched her nipples. Warm, questing fingertips played with one cresting peak, while the second one was subject to the cold glide of slowly melting ice.

His breath was hot against her face.

Then his hot mouth replaced the ice, sucking her nipple deep into the cavernous warmth.

She jerked as he transferred the ice to the other breast and rubbed its cold, hard surface against her soft warmth. Back and forth, breast to breast, he alternated his mouth and the ice.

"You're so hot," he murmured.

"Oh, that's cold," she said as he pressed the ice against the top of her bare thighs.

She heard him change positions and guessed he now knelt before her. He continued to ply the ice on her soft inner thigh, alternating with the heat of his mouth as he licked and nibbled, then jolted her with cold.

She bit her lip to avoid squealing aloud as she concentrated on the sensations flowing through her.

The rise and fall of her breathing sounded overloud in the silence, punctuated by the occasional whisper of silk and Sloan's sensuous murmurs against her skin. He raised her legs to rest atop his shoulders, then she felt his breath against her thigh, her inner lips, followed by the lash of his tongue.

"Oh!" It was both a prayer of thanks and a plea for more, cut short by the hit of ice, the burst of heat, a temperature duel of extremes. She was filled with heat, suffused with cold, melting, writhing, as tongue and ice cube warred for the prize and the power of heat reigned supreme.

"It didn't take long for that to melt."

His tongue darted in and out, stoking the flames of desire to unscaled heights. Lips, thumb, and tongue worked together, a contrast of texture, temperature, and pressure that sent her skyrocketing. He stayed with her through the explosion, his mouth gentle, soothing, then bringing her gently back to earth.

"How can I see fireworks when I can't see?"

"I bring the heavens down to you." His lips met hers.

"Is that me I taste?" she said.

"The world's sweetest nectar. Lie back."

He placed something beneath her head, probably his bundled-up jacket. When she reached for him, he caught her hand and closed it around his hot, throbbing length.

"Where's that ice when I need it?" she teased as she stroked him from root to tip. She heard his breath whistle between his teeth as she rolled the velvety tip in her palm. She guided it to her own body where she deliberately wielded it for her own pleasure, dampening him with the dew of her desire as she traced her inner shape and circled her sensitive pleasure pearl, rewarded by a fresh surge of lubricating dampness. She swore she could feel her insides swell, eager for that sweet first thrust, awash in desire to possess him.

He entered her slightly, withdrew, went a little deeper, and withdrew again. When he came back a third time, her hips were raised to sheath him fully.

"Oh!" She gave a cry of satisfaction as he filled her. "Yes!"

As their mouths fused she tightened her inner muscles, increasing the friction of his rhythm. When her next orgasm hit, she screamed, then grasped his hips, meeting him with an intense thrust of her own.

There was no slow buildup, no advance warning of the quake that burst free. She didn't know if her orgasm triggered his, or his triggered hers; she'd never experienced such intense release, heightened by the rightness of their joining.

Chapter Eight

Despite Sloan's arm around her waist, Cassidy sensed his withdrawal with each step closer to her suite. The closeness they'd achieved had been too close for his comfort zone; exactly as she had planned.

"You okay?" he asked as they reached her door.

She reminded herself to give him his space. "Never better." She gripped the front of his jacket and tilted her face up for his kiss, then drew back, releasing her hold on him. "I'll never forget dinner in Paris."

"Me either. Sweet dreams." He pressed a kiss to her forehead, shoved his hands in his pockets, and made his escape.

He knew that she stood in the doorway watching him and every time he left her seemed more difficult than the time before. Especially when the only beast he really needed to save Cassidy from was himself.

Inside his cabin, he splashed cold water on his face and stared into the mirror over the sink. Why wasn't he tired?

"Damn body clock must be all screwed up." His jacket smelled like Cassidy and he balled it up and tossed it in the cleaning bag for the steward, knowing as he did so that he'd never forget a single detail. Not the way she smelled, the way she felt, or the way she screamed his name in the heat of the moment.

Once he'd pulled on a clean shirt and jacket, he set off to discover how the night owls spent their time onboard ship. First he stopped into the disco for a drink, and let himself be dragged up onto the dance floor by two tipsy blondes. The strobe lights and loud music gave him a skuller of a headache and he lit out as soon as he could manage, much to the disappointment of his new friends, who hinted they'd be more than happy to get into a three-way encounter with him.

Since he didn't feel like family chitchat, he avoided the casino. Maybe a swim or a few rounds in the gym would help tire him out. But he knew nothing would quiet the thoughts whirling around in his head.

Eventually he found his way to the library. Perhaps delving into a book would do the trick.

He stopped short at the sight of his sister-in-law, Montana, the last person he expected to find awake. The light from a crook-neck reading lamp bathed her in a golden glow and she looked totally serene, some multicolored knitting resting on her pregnant belly.

He made his way to her side. "You shouldn't be up this late."

"Don't worry, I've been napping every day. The baby's restless and I didn't want to disturb Steele. What's your excuse?"

He slid into the upholstered high-backed chair across from her. "I'm not used to this vacation stuff. It's thrown my body clock off."

"Any chance that a certain redhead is responsible for your insomnia?"

"Cassidy's cool to hang with. That's all."

Montana nodded, plying her needles smoothly through the colorful yarn. She laughed when his jaw dropped at the sight of her stomach heaving and undulating all by itself. "I think the baby has its days and nights mixed up. It feels like dancing."

"Wow!" Sloan couldn't look away. "I hadn't thought of it as an individual with feelings and desires."

Montana took his hand and laid it on her stomach. "Bond with your niece or nephew. Talk to him so he recognizes your voice."

He jerked his hand back as if burned. "Did it just kick me?"

Montana laughed softly. "Maybe you deserve a good swift kick."

"What's that supposed to mean?"

Montana gave him a pitying look. "Are all men so dense,

or just Hardt males? It's obvious that you and Cassidy have a special connection."

"We've known each other a long time."

"What's that got to do with here and now?"

Sloan shifted in his chair, which felt like a hot seat. "Things are complicated."

"They were with Steele and me, too. We worked it out."

"For one thing, she's got some guy back home who wants to marry her."

"No surprise there. She's not with him, though, is she?"

"Her life is in West Bend. Mine's at Black Creek."

Montana merely lifted her brow.

"She wants kids and I'm not having any."

"Methinks the man doth protest a little too much."

"She just wants one last fling before she settles down. I'm accommodating her."

"You mean, she *says* that's what she wants."

"She was very clear about it from the beginning."

"And what about you? What do you want?"

He jumped to his feet. "What I *really* want is to get off this floating hotel and back to work."

Montana tsked as she knitted. "I thought you were the easygoing brother."

"I am."

"So why are you making things seem so difficult? Do whatever feels right and you'll be fine. Just don't run away from your feelings."

Easy for her to talk, Sloan thought as he paced the ship's promenade deck. Sitting there complacently, her life all smooth and settled. Of course, it hadn't been like that when he'd first met her. She had been struggling to get Black Creek's spa up and running; playing cat and mouse with Steele, who was giving her grief and spying on behalf of her investors, or something. He'd never gotten the whole story and it really didn't matter, for it had all turned out fine in the end.

The spa was wildly successful. Montana had tamed the wild Steele, who had taken to married life like a duck takes to water. Closer to home, Gramps was happy and his own parents were ecstatic. Even Montana's meddling mother-in-law was off on an extended honeymoon with her new husband.

Sloan leaned against the rail and stared into the inky blackness, lit by thousands of twinkling stars. In the distance winked a cluster of lights, one of the islands they were scheduled to explore tomorrow.

Maybe he lacked the fall-in-love-and-live-happily-ever-after gene. He liked being solo. Though he enjoyed female attention when it came his way, he didn't seek it out. He liked his own company too much to imagine having to put someone else first. He loved the option of saddling up and riding off whichever way the wind blew him, staying out there for as long as he felt like it.

As long as a woman accepted him that way, both parties could have a good time. At least, that's how it had always worked in the past. Why did this time feel different?

It would be far better for Cassidy to settle down with Mr. Safe and pop out a passel of kids. The life she longed for would never suit him.

He returned to Cassidy's cabin, used the key he still had to unlock the door, and padded silently through the darkened room, dropping his clothes as he went. He reached the bed and slid in next to Cassidy, being careful not to wake her. She stirred and rolled toward him, murmuring something unintelligible.

He wrapped himself around her and held her, hearing her breathing deepen as sleep reclaimed her. He was one damn selfish bastard, all right. But at least now he might be able to sleep.

It seemed like he'd no sooner fallen asleep than Cassidy was awake, jumping around like a kid on Christmas morning as she wrapped herself in a robe and stepped out onto the balcony. She didn't even seem surprised to see him, just accepted his presence as the most natural thing in the world. Was she used to falling asleep alone and waking up with company?

"Oh, Sloan, how pretty everything looks! I can't wait to go ashore."

The phone rang while he was struggling to wake up. She scampered in and grabbed it on the first ring.

"Hi, Mom. Sure. What time?" She winked at Sloan. "I'll tell him if I see him." She hung up and flashed him a naughty grin. "Your grandfather is looking for you. He wants to fill you in on what we're doing today."

"I know what I'd like to be doing today." He reached for her and caught the corner of her robe, but she pulled away.

"I'm having a shower."

He let her go first, stretched out in that comfy queen-size bed with his hands pillowed beneath his head, visualizing her all warm and wet. . . . He jackknifed out of bed. The bathroom door was ajar, and he didn't need any further invitation.

He heard Cass singing over the sound of the water; she sounded happy.

So was he, he realized with a jolt. Happier than he recalled being in a hell of a long time. When he opened the glass shower door she spun to face him, her open mouth another invitation, he decided, as he swooped in for a kiss.

She wrapped her slick arms around his neck. "What took you so long?"

"I didn't know if you might have girl things to take care of first."

"That's very thoughtful."

"I try."

She reached for his cock with a soap-slippery hand. "Try harder."

"One good thing about the mornings," he said. "He needs very little encouragement to rise to the occasion."

Sure enough, her lightest touch more than got the job done as he reached to cup her breasts in his palms. It was like a kick in the solar plexus. The way she tilted her pelvis, brushed herself teasingly against his hard-on, the short curls a further enticement to a crazy shower with jets of water coming at them from all directions.

"God, Cassidy!" He'd never gone from zero to full bore so fast. He was breathing hard as she beat him at his own game, gliding her hot, hungry hands over his body.

"Unfortunately, I think it needs to be a quickie," she murmured against his lips.

"Yeah!" His voice came out a growl.

The shower had a bench in one corner and he swiftly sat, pulled her onto his lap, then slid into her so deeply he thought he was going to lose it on the first pass.

Her groan of ecstasy heightened his excitement, the shower spray a background concerto. Her breasts brushed his chest and bobbed delightfully near as she rode him, her hardened nipples like points of fresh, sweet sensation.

He dragged his hands through her wet hair and plundered her mouth. She planted her feet against the wall behind him for leverage, increasing the frenzy with which she rode him. He stole her breath as hers increased to match his, one sweet tangle of wet, pulsing warmth.

He felt her start to quake deep within and tried to hold off his own pleasure, but when she came, so did he. On and on and on, in a swell of passion that never seemed like it was ever going to end. And damn, he wished it wouldn't.

He was far from recovered when she glanced at the face of his waterproof watch. "Lord, look at the time!" She eased off him, gave herself a quick dainty spray, then turned off that nice warm water. "Hurry up, we're going to be late."

"Apparently I need a longer recovery time than you do."

"Not you, who boasted about your recovery many a time," she teased.

"It's a boast I'll happily prove, as soon as you give me the chance," he invited.

"Right now, I want to see just how fast you can get into your clothes."

"Spoilsport," he groused good-naturedly.

A family junket had been arranged; an open-top Volkswagen bus piloted by a colorful local waited at the dock to tour them around the island.

They jounced along dusty gravel roads lined with lush vegetation and roadside stands selling everything from fresh fruit and fish to trashy trinkets and real art and jewelry. Their driver honked as they passed a dark-skinned man with a youngster riding high atop his shoulders. The kid smiled and waved, while the father gave them a gleaming face-splitting grin.

The people didn't seem to have much but they sure seemed content, Sloan thought. Maybe they had it figured out. A little piece of paradise, simple life, simple pleasures. The industrialized world might not be so smart after all.

The womenfolk sat up front to chatter to the driver, while the men took up the rear. Cassidy was eye-catching in her short halter dress in brilliant jungle tones.

Sloan caught a glimpse of his brother's scowling mug and moved to sit next to him. "You look like you're at a funeral instead of a wedding party. What's up?"

Steele's gaze flicked to Montana, talking to Angel and the others at the front of the bus.

"We almost didn't come today. Though she denies it, I know Montana's not feeling a hundred percent."

"Probably the heat," Sloan said.

"Maybe," Steele said. "I wanted the two of us to stay behind, but she couldn't bear to disappoint Mom."

"I ran into her late last night in the library. She seemed to be feeling okay."

"She's always thinking about everyone else. The latest thing she's on about is you and Cassidy, wondering what we can do."

"I wish people would get off that. We're friends, and that's how it stays."

"Montana's got it wrong then?"

Sloan smiled at the memory of the beauty salon. "I'm only doing what you said I should do."

"Since when do you listen to anything I say?" Steele gave him the elbow. "I'd get up there and do some serious damage control, if I were you."

The road ahead petered out into a parking lot. With an ear-splitting grind of gears, their vehicle lumbered to a stop. The dusty lot was half-full of vehicles, from tin-can-size rentals cars to large tour buses.

"What is this place?" Sloan asked Steele.

"Some tourist attraction. Waterfalls, caves. It's where they shot scenes from one of the Tarzan movies, I think."

Once disembarked, their group scattered, some to the restrooms, others to the bar or gift shops as the driver told them they had two hours to have lunch and explore.

Sloan caught up with Cassidy and touched her bare shoulder. "Did you bring any sunblock? It looks like you missed a spot."

"Really?" She fished in her bag and pulled out a camera, a bottle of water, a map, a towel, and finally a tube of lotion.

He squirted lotion into his palm to warm it, then slowly rubbed it into her skin, paying special attention to the back of her neck, the sweet curve of neck to shoulder, and the lobes of her ears. He felt a tiny shiver ripple through her, heard her breath catch before he leaned forward.

"That was fun in the shower this morning," he murmured in her ear. He loved making her blush.

"We almost missed the tour."

"Would that have been so bad?" His hands skimmed around to the front of her, ostensibly applying lotion to her chest, lingering on the soft swell of her breasts where they peeked from the neckline of her halter dress.

With a graceful sway she leaned back against him, her body melting into his, her bare neck begging for his kiss. He obliged as he pulled her tight against him, teasing her with his instant response to her nearness.

"Sloan, we're out in the open."

"It didn't bother you in the pool the other night."

"That was different. It was dark."

"And we almost got busted."

"Almost." She smiled at the memory.

Following his instinct, Sloan beelined for the shallow river and headed upstream, keeping firm hold of Cassidy even as he slowed his pace to match hers in those flimsy flip-flops women seemed to favor.

"Do you know where you're going?" she asked.

"We'll soon find out."

Their surroundings really were like something from a tourist's guidebook. Smooth rocks stuck out of the shallow water, nature's bridge to the other side. Vegetation was lush and green, sprinkled with exotic blooms, and nearby tree branches were home to wild-colored, noisy birds.

"Look!" Cassidy exclaimed as they rounded a bend and stopped. A picturesque waterfall spilled into a swimming hole. Birds sang and sunlight created rainbow prisms through the waterfall mist.

"It's like a movie set," Cassidy said as she dug out her camera and started to click away.

"Apparently it was, a long time ago. Let me get a picture of you. Drop your bag on the sand and then stand over there."

"How's this?"

He frowned and squinted into the camera. "Back. Back farther. A bit more— Got it." He snapped the shutter just as Cassidy lost her footing and went over backward with a splash.

"You did that on purpose!" She grabbed her floating straw hat and tossed it ashore.

He grinned. "A small sacrifice for art—it was a great action shot." He tucked the camera back in her bag. "How's the water?"

"Come in and see."

He peeled off his shirt, dropped it on top of her bag, and prepared to dive in.

"Don't!" she shrieked. "It's too shallow."

But her words came too late. Down he dove. And stayed there, counting silently, knowing Cassidy wouldn't let him down.

She swam toward where he lay unmoving on the shallow bottom. Just as she reached him he sprang into action, grabbed her, and pulled her back to the surface.

"You wretch, you scared me half to death!" She struck out as if to hit him. He caught her arm and their tussle became a seductive water dance as he edged them toward the waterfall, just close enough to have their skin kissed with droplets of overspray.

He planted his feet firmly on the sandy river bottom at the point where the water was just past his waist and nearly up to Cassidy's chest.

He tugged the skimpy tie of her halter, then helped her dress float free of her. "Have you skinny-dipped since that time you and I—?"

"Other than in the pool?" She shook her head, her hands resting on his shoulders as her panties went the way of her dress, which he tossed onto shore along with his board shorts.

When he pulled her flush against him, they sighed in unison at the raw sensuality of it; the warm water caressing their skin, the background symphony of the waterfall.

"This is amazing," she breathed.

He kissed her, running his hands freely over her body underwater.

"Sloan." She glanced around. "Someone might come 'round that corner any time."

"They might." His hand was busy between her legs, seeking her inner heat, enjoying the responsive way she swelled and unfolded against him. His other hand paid homage to her breasts, felt the way her nipples crested eagerly in his palm. He ducked his head for a taste, tugged the tight, tasty bud deep into his mouth, and lashed it with his tongue. He felt a rush of heat against his other hand as her body dampened in welcome.

Teeth bared, he lightly nipped her nipple as he tweaked the swollen bud of her clitoris.

"Oh God!" She tossed back her head and let the orgasm shudder through her.

" 'Oh God' or 'oh good'?" he asked.

"Both." Her voice was a throaty purr of satisfaction and he took advantage of her relaxed state to lift her legs around his waist, his cock rooting for her opening.

"Sloan." Her fingers clutched his shoulders, plucking frantically. "We can't."

"There's no such thing as can't."

She opened her eyes wide as his cock slid into her and their bodies effortlessly found that age-old rhythm as he flexed and thrust on his way to filling her.

He felt the way she adjusted her perch atop him, ensuring her clit got maximum friction as he increased the pace.

She reached around and gently fondled his balls before she moved past and found his special sweet spot, the seam between his scrotum and ass.

His breath hissed between his teeth as he felt her inner muscles tighten and clench, squeezing him so tight he could barely move.

He felt her starting to come again and it seemed she was determined this time to take him with her. He fondled her ass and rubbed his chest back and forth against her wet breasts, the hard tips of her nipples making his cock even harder.

He managed to hold off, loving to watch her come, eyes at dreamy half-mast, mouth all soft and kissable, seconds before everything exploded. Her legs went tense; then her body arched away from his as if she were the bow and he were her arrow.

He felt the aftershocks ripple through her and sipped at her lips, tasting the sweetness of her ecstasy burn through her and enter his bloodstream.

She rested, soft and pliant in his arms, and he took delight in renewing his efforts to rekindle the flames. Then she fisted his cock between them, stroking it in tandem with his thrusts. "I hear someone coming," she whispered in his ear.

"Too bad." He couldn't stop now if he had to. She slid her baby finger into his rear opening and, blindsided by her tactics, his explosion took them both. Somehow he managed to stagger beneath the waterfall with her in his arms, where the pound of water added to the impact, and he only hoped the noise muffled his hoarse cry.

Cassidy wrapped herself around him as he caught his breath. When he caught sight of her self-satisfied smile, he sensed something was up.

"What's that smile all about?"

"When I said someone was coming? I made that up."

Chapter Nine

"What!"

"You have to admit, it added to the excitement." She grinned as she slowly unwrapped herself from him.

"Finished with me already?" he teased.

"For now," she flung over her shoulder as she waded to shore, spread her towel on the sand, and reclined back on her elbows, watching as Sloan made his way toward her like some gift from the water gods. Sunlight glistened on the water that clung to his tanned, muscular torso and shoulders and she didn't feel the least bit shy as he stopped a few feet away and looked his fill.

"No longer worried about voyeurs, I see."

"Funny, how you manage to peel away my inhibitions. But you always did have that knack."

He squatted at her feet. "Glad I haven't lost it. Judging by your tan lines, this is your first time nude sunbathing." He traced the band of pale skin crossing her breasts, then outlined her Venus triangle. "I recommend a healthy dose of SPF thirty everywhere."

She tossed him the tube of lotion and rolled onto her stomach.

"Whoa, let me grab my sunglasses. You are blindingly white." As he smoothed cream over her derriere and the backs of her thighs, she parted her legs slightly and felt the obliging pressure of his fingers glide toward her front opening.

She pillowed her face on her arms. "The sun feels good."

"Only the sun?"

"Maybe not *only* the sun."

He hooked an arm under her waist and turned her over effortlessly. Then he bent her knees, exposing her to the sunlight and his view as he massaged lotion into the insides of her thighs.

She sighed. "Positively hedonistic."

As he leaned forward and lightly applied sun lotion to her breasts, she sighed her pleasure.

He stretched out atop her and rubbed her body with his so her breasts were alternately tickled and stimulated by the whisk of chest hair. "I thought we'd share the lotion."

"Good idea." She clutched his upper arms, absorbed the powerful flex of muscles as he supported part of his body weight above her. Before she could get too enthralled, he glided down her length, leaving her exposed to the sun, to his burning gaze.

As she tried to decide which had more heat, he dipped his head and drank in her essence. She was already supersensitive from their earlier escapades so he used the lightest tongue play, the barest whisper of his lips across hers, his tongue lightly separating the tender folds before he honed in on the jewel in the crown. She arched against him as he lightly dragged his mouth from inner thigh to inner thigh, lingering over the junction, a delicate tasting, as he breathed in her special flavor.

The overhead sky was an intense blue, seeming heightened by the intense sensations Sloan awoke inside her. Cassidy reached down and ran her fingers through his damp hair, sifting its silky strands between her fingers, feeling a pleasurable tightening low in her belly.

"Do your breasts like the sun?" he asked.

"All of me likes the sun."

"Good. Feel it." He pulled back just as she was on the brink. She felt an empty throb at the sudden lack of fulfillment, Sloan's tongue replaced by the sun's kiss.

"Finish it," he said huskily. "I want to watch you pleasure yourself."

She glanced around. "What if someone comes?"

"We're all alone in Eden."

She couldn't deny the rush of excitement at his suggestion. The throbbing between her legs intensified; her breasts burned for attention as the sun's heat heightened her own flaming need.

She started with her breasts, trailing her fingertips across their rounded contours.

"Does that feel good?" Sloan said.

"Mmmmm," she said dreamily. She only had to tweak her nipples to feel the resurgence deep within.

She licked her fingertips and played their cool dampness against her sun-kissed skin. Slowly she stroked her inner thighs, feeling the incredible softness of her skin.

Then she dipped her middle finger across her inner lips, where damp heat dewed her fingers. Her inner lips felt plump, swollen and hot.

Sloan's blue eyes darkened, his breath quickened, and her excitement grew as she realized she was turning him on. She used her other hand to play with her breasts as she increased the pressure and intensity against her swollen love knot, moaning as waves of pleasure rolled through her. She dipped her middle finger inside again and again, then returned her attentions to her clitoris, feeling it swell, everything damp and hot.

As hot as Sloan's gaze. His cock was hard and she licked her lips, imagining its velvety hardness against her lips. Faster she rubbed, her panting moans nearly drowning out Sloan's heavy breathing, till she arched up with a triumphant cry of release.

Sloan lunged forward and buried himself inside her. Her trill of pleasure at their joining was pure ecstasy, ringing through the stillness. She grabbed him and held on tight, determined to never let go.

"Yes!" Matching her frantic need, he plunged into her

with driving intent, each thrust harder and more powerful, spiraling her up into mindless pleasure where nothing existed save the two of them.

Afterward he lay spent atop her, his body giving an occasional twitch as the aftershocks ran through him. She smoothed his back, felt the kiss of the sun's warmth on his skin and hers, thrilled that she could affect him as deeply as he touched her.

With a weighty sigh, he heaved himself up to sprawl next to her, his arm across his eyes. She draped herself across his chest and tugged playfully on the hair there, then lightly tickled him between his hip bone and the top of his thigh, smiling when he jumped reactively.

"Are you going to survive?" she asked.

"Not sure," he mumbled into his arm. "Now I know what they mean by 'fuck me dead.' "

She glanced around, basking in the tropical glory of their surroundings. "I like making love outdoors."

"I like making love with you." He got to his feet, scooped her into his arms, and waded into the water, then ducked down till the water hit their chins.

Teasingly, she reached down and pretended to wash him. Sloan shook his head, spun in a circle to distract her, then headed back to shore, where they toweled each other dry and dressed.

"I'll get it." Sloan saw her struggle with the halter tie of her dress before he pushed her hands away and secured the garment. "I guess we'd better get back before they send out a search party."

They found Rake and Angel with James and Louise in the restaurant, a spacious open-air room with cool tile floors, lazy ceiling fans, dark rough-hewn furniture, and beams set against plaster walls inset with tiles. Everywhere Cassidy looked she saw exotic blooming plants as birds flew in freely, looking for crumbs.

"Where have you two been?" Angel asked.

"Exploring," Sloan said.

"So that's what they're calling it these days." At Angel's tinkling laugh, Cassidy felt the heat of her give-away blush, although Sloan appeared unaffected. No doubt he was used to the teasing.

"Yum!" She dove into the plate of deep-friend calamari, glad for the distraction.

"Hungry?" Rake asked.

"Starving," Cassidy said, reaching for a second piece. "Has everyone else eaten?"

James signaled to the waiter, who ambled over to take Cassidy's and Sloan's lunch orders.

Sloan glanced around. "Where are Steele and Montana?"

"They went back to the ship," Angel said. "I think Montana is more tired than she's letting on." She tugged Rake to his feet. "Let's go take a few more pictures before we go. This is our last ever honeymoon."

"There's a really pretty waterfall not far upstream," Cassidy said. "Sloan and I, um, went for a quick swim."

"This is a fabulous spot," Louise said. "I've never been on a cruise before, and pleasant as it is, I do prefer being on firm land."

The waiter quickly delivered their meals, breaded and pan-fried catch of the day with sweet potato fries.

Louise smiled as Cassidy tucked in. "I don't think I've ever seen you eat so much at one sitting." She bit off her words. "Sorry, I didn't mean to . . ."

"It's okay, Mom." Cassidy reached across and patted her mother's hand. "I have a healthy relationship with food these days. Sloan says I was 'pleasingly plump,' but it wasn't pleasing to me. Especially since I mostly ate because I was unhappy." They all knew she referred to her bullying father. "In an effort to lose the weight, I developed an eating disorder. But I'm fine now, happy and healthy. My mom just worries."

"As is every mother's right," Louise interjected.

"Well, I now know to stop eating once I'm full and I promise not to go throw it up. Okay, Mom?"

Louise nodded. "It was a very scary time. And I blame myself."

"There's no laying blame," Cassidy said.

Louise nodded. "I'm just so happy, I want the same for my little girl."

"I'm not a little girl, Mom." Cassidy shook her head with a smile.

"You will always be my little girl. You'll understand once you have your own child."

Anytime she thought about having a child, it always had Sloan's mesmerizing blue eyes. "Excuse me. I need to go to the ladies' room."

Louise rose. "I'll come with you."

"Never knew a woman to go to the ladies' room by herself if there was another woman in the vicinity," James said with an indulgent smile.

"Tell me you didn't follow along to check on me," Cassidy said as she washed her hands and touched up her lip gloss.

"Of course not," Louise said. "I actually was curious to know if you've seen any of the fantasy suites on the ship."

Cassidy went rigid. "What do you know about the fantasy suites?"

"Not much," Louise said. "That's why I'm curious. James surprised me by booking some for us, but I thought it was a silly thing at our age and suggested he pass the keys along to Sloan."

"As far as I know, Sloan still has the keys," Cassidy said stiffly. "You should check it out. Who knows when you'll get the opportunity again?"

"I'm sorry I said something wrong," Louise said, eyes wide with concern. "I didn't mean to."

"Mom, you and I agreed a long time ago that we could tell each other anything. You didn't say anything wrong. Quit worrying."

"I know you, Cassidy. You're holding something back."

"Everything's fine, really. I think I got a bit too much sun, is all."

She followed her mother back to their table, her eyes on Sloan. She still hadn't brought him to his knees, which meant it was time for more drastic measures.

"Looks like it's time to head off." James dropped some money onto the table and stood next to Louise.

"We'll see you at the bus," Sloan said. As soon as they

left, he turned to Cassidy. "Did something happen back there in the washroom? You seem different."

"We can talk about it later."

"Okay." Sloan snagged a few sweet potato fries from Cassidy's plate and stood. "You ready?"

She nodded and made her way ahead of him through the restaurant, her spine ramrod stiff, her steps ringing against the tile floor in a way that told him something was definitely eating her. Being female, she no doubt expected him to intuitively know what was bugging her. Well, damned if he was going to ask a second time. She'd bring it up when it suited her. Women always did.

When their group piled back onto the open-air tour bus he lost Cassidy, or she deliberately lost him, wedged in at the very back, admiring others' souvenir purchases.

Okay, so he wasn't imagining the cold shoulder. He plunked down near his folks and did his best to appreciate their enthusiasm for the night ahead, which they told him included a Vegas-style stage performance.

"I'd have thought you'd be tired of that kind of thing," he asked.

Rake linked his fingers with Angel's. "When you live in Vegas, you don't experience it the same way as the tourists. We never go to the shows."

Angel spoke up. "We wanted you and Steele to have as normal an upbringing as possible, but it was a tough decision to leave you at the ranch with your grandfather."

"And here I thought we were just cramping your swinging party lifestyle."

Was that a sudden sheen of tears in his mother's blue eyes? "It wasn't like that at all. Neither of us knew how to make a living outside the city, but we could see Vegas wasn't good for you boys. You both came to life when we visited the ranch. Horses, dogs, fishing . . . all the things a boy needs. We wanted you to have all those things."

"So you left us with Gramps." He realized how bitter he sounded, about stuff he thought he'd come to terms with a long time ago. He even enjoyed himself the odd time he went to Vegas.

Her voice caught. "It was the hardest decision we ever made."

His father nodded. "It tore your mother apart every time we went to see you and then had to leave you all over again."

Sloan shifted. "I never knew that. I only knew you guys were getting divorced."

His mother reached for his hand. "You knew we loved you."

"I guess." He'd always wondered how they could have just dropped him and Steele off like a couple of puppies they'd gotten tired of, once they'd outgrown the cute stage.

Past hurts, that long-ago feeling of abandonment he thought he'd outgrown, welled up inside him. "Maybe you should have thought it through a little more before you had kids."

"Every parent does their best, Sloan. One day you'll understand what I mean," Angel said.

"Not me." He looked past her at the passing scenery, which was a blur of green. "I'm not having kids."

"You'll change your mind when you meet the right woman."

He folded his arms over his chest and his mom seemed to get the hint that the topic was now closed.

It could have been his imagination, but it felt like Cassidy deliberately gave him the slip as their group boarded the ship. Did she really think she could dodge him for the rest of the cruise?

He caught up with her as she unlocked the door to her suite. "Where have you been?"

He saw her shoulders rise defensively before she turned to face him. "I was checking on Montana. If you weren't so self-involved, you'd have figured that out by yourself."

Ouch. "How is she?"

"She's okay. Her blood pressure is up a bit, but nothing alarming. She's not one to rest though, is she?"

"She's a doer. Nothing is likely to piss her off more than feeling she needs mollycoddling."

"She just needs to practice going slower."

"I hope you told her that."

"She knows."

"Well, there's a few things I'd like to know. Like what pissed you off back at the restaurant?"

She faced him down, a stubborn look on her face that he knew well. "Go away, Sloan. I don't want to talk to you."

He leaned against the wall, arms folded across his chest. "That's adult of you."

"You don't get it. You'll never get it." She tried to slip inside, but he pushed in behind her.

"I'm trying to get it. You're not making it easy."

She dropped her beach bag on the bench at the end of the bed. "You, of all people, ought to understand."

He raked his fingers through his hair. "Understand what, for God's sake? Help me out here."

"You know how I grew up, with my mother scared to death of my father. He abused her and when that got boring he started on me. Do you know why I became a midwife?"

Sloan shook his head, trying to follow her thought process.

"He said I was too homely to get a man and have my own family, so I might as well make a career out of looking after other people's."

"Your father was one sick bastard."

"Yes, he was. And my mother was terrified of him, but she wouldn't leave him. She didn't have enough self-esteem to think she could make it on her own."

Sloan still wasn't following what seemed completely obvious to Cassidy.

"I spent my entire life determined not to be like that. Not to follow in those footsteps."

"Uh-huh." He tried to sound sympathetic but damn it, what did one thing have to do with the other?

"And then, there you go! You inherit some secret male rites of passage from your grandfather, so that I have the fantasy suites experience intended for my mother."

Sloan frowned in confusion. "Cassidy, it's not like that."

"No one is turning me into my mother, Sloan. Especially not you."

"Cass, you came after *me,* remember?"

She blew out her breath. "Our arrangement is null and void."

"We have two more days together," he protested.

"Not anymore. As of here and now, we're done."

Chapter Ten

Cassidy paced the cabin, the sound of Sloan slamming the door still ringing in her ears. She'd been so intent on bringing Sloan to his knees, ensuring he fell in love with her so she could teach him a lesson on behalf of all the heartbroken women in his wake that she'd failed to notice she'd fallen in love with *him*!

God, she was no different from all those other women who'd fallen for that famous Hardt charm. Her excuse for calling it quits between them was weak, she knew, but at this point it was all about survival. She couldn't have Sloan guess the truth. So she couldn't spend more time with him.

She wanted what Montana had, complete with a baby moving inside her while her husband hovered close by, the love he felt for his wife obvious to everyone.

She knew Sloan's happy-go-lucky banter hid a wide stubborn streak, and no matter how much he denied it, Big Brother Steele had been a tough act to follow.

Even as kids, whatever Steele did, Sloan did a wide one-eighty to prove he was different. Every bit as good, as successful, as right in his choices; a pattern too ingrained to ever change. So with Steele happily married, Sloan would remain a confirmed bachelor.

She couldn't abandon her dreams of a family, Playfair House, and the chance to make a difference in other people's lives, to have half a life with Sloan. Eventually she'd end up resenting him and hating herself for making those sacrifices.

Her mother had finally found happiness, but for as long as Cassidy could remember growing up, she'd been a broken shadow, bereft of all passion and dreams. Cassidy wanted more.

It wasn't too difficult to stay out of Sloan's way for the rest of the cruise. The family seemed to sense something was up and although no one said a word, she felt them close ranks protectively, somehow sensing that she and Sloan needed this time apart. Occasionally she'd look up and find her mother's thoughtful gaze upon her, at which point she would force a cheery smile and retreat into her book.

After two long, lonely, and painful days, the ship finally docked. She was conscious of Sloan in the background as everyone said their good-byes, the wedding guests scattering to various departure flights, and Angel and Rake continuing on the next leg of their honeymoon.

"Keep an eye on this girl," Cassidy told Steele as she and Montana said their farewells. "Make sure she doesn't do too much when you get back to Black Creek."

Steele gave a lazy grin. "Sounds like a good excuse to tie her to the bed."

Montana lit right up. "Again?" she teased.

Cassidy turned away from the intimate exchange, hoping her envy didn't show. What she wouldn't give to be part of such a secure, happy, and intimate relationship.

Her move brought her face-to-face with Sloan. Flustered, she stuck out her hand. "Good to reconnect."

He stared hard at her hand till it fell limply between them. She was still trying to decide what to do when he gathered her close for a hug. "I think we moved past the hand-shaking stage a while back."

She couldn't stop herself from melting against him, knowing this well could be the last time they touched.

She patted his cheek. "We'll always have Paris."

He smiled down at her, a slow, intimate smile that warmed the coldest, deepest part of her, the part that was trying desperately to stay detached. "That we will."

She was glad to hear Steele say, "Hey, Sloan, they're calling our flight." And just like that, he was gone.

Sitting in the airport with James and her mother, she suddenly couldn't wait to get home. Back to West Bend. Back to normal. Back to the patiently waiting Tony.

"What the hell happened between you and Cass?"

Sloan sighed aloud. "Montana, will you call him off?"

She leaned forward to look past Steele, across the aisle at him. "I'm waiting to hear what you have to say for yourself."

"It was only an onboard fling."

"Was it my imagination, or did she end the fling early?" Montana asked.

Sloan wished he could disappear into his seat. "Define 'early.' "

"What happened?"

God, she was worse than Steele. "How would I know? All of a sudden she was on with some trumped-up excuse about me trying to turn her into her mother."

"Ah. It's very unsettling for a woman to see bits of her mother's character traits, usually the ones she likes least, appear in herself."

"That's the dumbest thing I ever heard," Sloan scoffed.

"Ask your brother. I was so determined not to turn out like my own mother, I did my best to drive him away because of it."

Sloan shook his head. "You women are way too complicated for me."

Montana poked Steele. "What would you do, Steele?"

"Leave her to stew a while, then casually look her up later?"

Montana gave him a pitying look. "Sloan, did you hear what your brother just said?"

"Yeah. And I know better than listen, 'cause as usual, he's way off base."

"Exactly."

Before Sloan could congratulate himself, she continued. "I bet if you flew Steele's plane from Black Creek to West Bend, you could beat her home."

Steele straightened. "Why would he want to do that?"

"Yeah," Sloan said. "Why would I want to do that?"

"If you want her, you need to show her that. Women love to be pursued."

Steele laughed, tipped his hat over his eyes, and reclined back in his seat. "Sloan's never pursued a woman in his life. He wouldn't know how."

"Maybe it's time he learned. After all, you did."

"How do you figure?"

"That PR stunt you pulled with the phony engagement?"

Steele smiled broadly. "You have to admit, that was clever."

"That was also when I knew just how serious you were," Montana said.

The wheels of the Falcon touched down on the landing strip at the Hardt family ranch with a "welcome back" thump. It hadn't been easy moving to Black Creek when his whole life had been spent here at West Bend, since it felt a bit like he was following Steele around. But Montana had offered him a challenge he was ready for, the chance to make his own mark, and he knew he'd done the right thing.

Gramps and Louise weren't back yet, so he borrowed one of the ranch's pickups and headed to town. Montana "just happened" to have Cassidy's address.

He found her tidy bungalow at the end of a dead-end street. The key was hidden predictably on the frame above the door, so he let himself in and made himself at home. The place was neat as a pin. Comfy, with lots of books, a few hearty-looking plants, and a piano in one corner. The couch was littered with cushions. Did all women deliberately make their homes soft, matching their own rounded curves? He found a beer at the back of the fridge and took it out to the front porch to wait.

He'd barely settled into the sturdy wooden rocker when a conservative gray sedan pulled to the curb. A man got out and started up the front walk. He was tall and thin with sparse brown hair and carried a bouquet of yellow roses. He hesitated when he saw Sloan's booted feet on the porch railing.

"I, uh . . ." He cleared his throat. "I was looking for Cassidy." He gestured to the curb. "I recognized James's truck and figured he'd dropped her off."

"She's not back yet," Sloan said comfortably. "Can I tell her who called?"

"It's uh, it's uh, Tony."

"A pleasure, Tony." He rose and took the bouquet from the other man. "Nice flowers. Let me put those in water." He tossed them carelessly onto a nearby stool.

Tony glanced from Sloan to the open front door, his confusion evident.

"I took a different flight back and beat them home," Sloan

continued conversationally, leaning one shoulder against a post, crossing his arms and his ankles as if he were there every day.

"You were on the cruise, too?"

"Yeah, son of the bride and groom and all. I kinda had to be there."

"I see." Tony started to edge away. "Tell Cassidy I'll call her later, okay?"

"Sure thing," Sloan said, thumbs hooked in his pockets. "See you around."

He resisted the temptation to chuck the roses in the trash, instead shoving them into an empty milk pitcher.

He was still inside when he heard a car pull into the attached garage. Cassidy came in the side door, dragging her suitcase behind her, and stopped short at the sight of him.

Sloan took the bag's handle from her unresisting hand. "Welcome home. Good flight?" He peered past her and added, "Nice car." In the garage was a totally impractical bright red Miata with its top down.

Cassidy dropped her purse on the table. "I thought I said good-bye to you already today."

"Turned out to be premature," he said.

"Nice flowers." She pushed past him and filled the kettle.

"Some dude named Tony. He the one?"

"What one?"

"The prospective father of your children?"

"He's asked me to marry him, if that's what you mean."

"Well, there's no way you're following in your mother's footsteps there. He's nothing like your old man."

"That's the idea."

"I'm getting that."

"Let's cut to the chase. Why are you here?" she asked.

"Well, it struck me that it's pretty hard to judge what a person's like when you're suspended from reality on one of those cruise ships. I thought I should see you in your true environment."

"You make it sound like a visit to the zoo," she said, pushing at her hair as if it irritated her.

The kettle shrilled. "I'll make you tea," Sloan offered. "Still an Earl Grey girl?"

She stared at him so long that he started to feel uncomfortable. He delved through the cupboards in search of a teapot. What had he thought? That he'd show up and she'd fly into his arms? Clearly that wasn't happening. In fact, she didn't seem pleased to see him at all. What had Montana said? Pursue her?

He summoned up his most persuasive grin. "I thought I'd see if I could take you out for dinner tonight."

"I've just returned from being away. The last thing I want is a restaurant meal."

"We'll eat in then," he said, proud of his solution.

"Great. You go get groceries. I'm going to take a long bath."

"What do you feel like cooking?"

"I don't." She took her cup of tea into the bathroom. He heard the loud *click* of the old-fashioned lock.

Cassidy sank down into the deep water of her old-fashioned claw-foot tub. Weren't you supposed to come back from a vacation refreshed and renewed?

It had been a mistake from the outset to tangle with

Sloan. She ought to have known that there was no way she could separate the physical from the emotional. Being intimate with him had fired up emotions from years ago and now they blazed inside of her.

On the other hand, since Sloan had shown up to woo her, she was halfway to bringing him to his knees. She'd reject him, he'd go away, and she would half win. Or would he dig in his heels? Didn't men always hanker after what they couldn't have?

The worst thing she could do was cave. Or was it? If Sloan only wanted her because he thought he couldn't have her. . . . She could turn it around and tell him she was all his. That ought to send him hightailing for cover double-time.

She pulled herself from the tub, as confused as ever. Maybe she ought to flip a coin. Heads, she stayed aloof and distant. Tails, she'd pretend he'd won her over.

She had a bad feeling it didn't matter which role she played.

Sloan wasn't good for her; they were oil and water. She might need to make him see that, so it became all his idea to leave.

The good and the bad thing about growing up on a ranch was that there was always someone else to do the cooking. Overwhelmed by the foreign territory of the market, he was reduced to a cheating phone call.

"Gramps. It's me. . . . Yeah, I figured you saw the plane. . . . Is Louise around? Can I please talk to her?"

Sloan unpacked the groceries he'd bought when, after her

initial reluctance to help him, Louise had turned into his guiding angel. Keep it simple, she'd said. Pasta. Garlic bread. Salad. Wine. Something even he ought to be able to handle. Besides, surely Cass would appreciate his efforts and chip in to help.

His mind conjured up an image of the two of them companionably cooking side by side. Except they weren't at her place in his visual, they were in his new house at Black Creek. It was a heartwarming picture that made him smile and he was still smiling when Cassidy appeared wrapped in a bathrobe.

"Good bath?" he asked, as if being in her kitchen unloading groceries was the most natural thing in the world.

"I thought you left."

"We needed a few groceries. And some black-eyed Susans."

Her gaze swung from him to the flowers and back to him. Score one for Louise!

"I saw their cheery faces and thought of you."

"They're my favorite."

Sloan smiled modestly. Maybe this wooing stuff wasn't so tough, after all.

He indicated the bathroom. "Okay if I catch a shower?"

"Help yourself."

"Why don't I pour you a glass of wine first?"

"That sounds lovely."

"A nice, simple Chianti," he said. "A taste of Italian sunshine in a glass."

Wine delivered, he slung his bag over his shoulder and closeted himself in the bathroom.

He stopped short at the sight of the claw-foot tub and turned back. "Cass, where's the shower?"

"It's handheld. It clips onto the tap."

What a stupid invention! Not only did the flimsy curtain not pull closed tightly, how were you supposed to soap and rinse with one hand holding the showerhead?

He still had suds clinging to him when he gave up and turned off the water. The bathroom looked like a pipe had burst, but he did a reasonable job of mopping up, even if he did use every towel in the place, bundling them into the tub when he was done.

He stepped out into the kitchen, expecting to smell the mingled flavors of garlic and tomato and basil. Instead, there was nothing.

"Cassidy?"

"In here."

He came to an abrupt stop in the living room doorway. For curled up on the couch was Cassidy, next to suitor Tony.

Chapter Eleven

"Sloan, you met Tony earlier today. And guess what?" Cassidy smiled sweetly. "Turns out he was free for dinner."

She almost laughed at the disgruntled expression on Sloan's face. His scowl deepened when he reached for the wine bottle, only to find it nearly empty.

Tony leapt to his feet. "I brought some wine. Let me get it."

"Tony has an amazing wine cellar," Cassidy said.

"It's a bit of a hobby," Tony said modestly. "I thought this Chateau LaTour would be perfectly suited to your return." He presented the bottle first to Cassidy, then to Sloan, like he was some damn sommelier in a fancy restaurant.

Cassidy examined the label and clapped her hands. "Lovely."

"Yeah, lovely," Sloan echoed, trying not to sound as surly as he felt.

"Sloan, sweetie," Cassidy purred, "there's some bruschetta mixed up in the fridge. Why don't you fix us some crostini while I show Tony the rest of the pictures from our cruise?"

"Some what?"

"You know, just toast some of that French bread you bought."

It sounded to him like she was trying to get rid of him. "That bread won't fit in the toaster, it's too small."

"Just lay it on a cookie sheet, brush it with olive oil, and slide it under the broiler."

"Nice of you to take care of the meal while Cassidy and I catch up," Tony had the nerve to say.

Sloan took a healthy slug of his wine, delighted to see the wine snob actually wince. "I'm just that kind of guy." He sloshed some more wine into his glass and headed for the kitchen, where he banged and crashed around so they didn't forget he was there. Finally he found a baking sheet, poured oil onto the bread, and slid it into the oven.

He inspected the garlic. Would two be enough? The recipe said two or three.

Might as well start dinner. He chopped up tomatoes for sauce and threw them into a pan along with the garlic and the basil, feeling quite domestic and proud of himself as he read the directions on the box of pasta.

The box didn't say anything about it boiling over,

though, and he watched in dismay as the water frothed out from under the lid and sizzled all over the stovetop.

"Sloan, what's burning?" Cassidy appeared in the doorway, then rushed past him and flung open the oven. Smoke billowed into the room.

"You're not supposed to put the loaf in whole. And you need to watch it so it doesn't burn." She grabbed a pot holder and threw the blacked mess into the garbage. "Have you ever cooked before?"

"I figure there's always a first time," he said with his best boyish charm. "And nothing I wouldn't do for you."

She peered into the sauce pan, where three bulbs of garlic bobbed in the sauce, and burst out laughing. "You're supposed to peel and mince the garlic. And use cloves, not entire heads." She forked a strand of pasta from the pot and bit into it. "How long has this been boiling?"

Sloan shrugged. "It was rock hard. I figured it would take a while to soften."

"You need to cook pasta just so."

"How do you get everything to finish at the same time?"

"Practice."

"There're other things I'd rather practice," he said huskily, pulling her to him. "Like us getting finished at the same time." He took a deep appreciative sniff of her hair. How did she get it to smell like flowers? She put her hands on his chest as if to push him away, yet wound up pulling him closer as he cupped the rounded curve of her ass, angling her against him. She arched her back, her pelvis locked with his, her eyes far too serious as they searched his face.

She felt like perfection in his arms. "I'd rather have you for dinner." He nuzzled her neck, blew on it, then tongued that sensitive cord at the side, feeling her go all soft and melty. Step by step, in a dance as old as mankind, he backed her over to the kitchen table and onto the smooth wooden surface.

He pushed her legs apart and stood at their juncture, rolling his hips from side to side against her. He could feel her heat, smell the intoxicating fragrance of her arousal, and his body reacted predictably.

"Tony," she whispered against his starved and ravaging mouth. "Tony's in the other room."

"Send him away." Sloan alternately sipped and nipped her sweetness, feeling the force of their combined desire flow from her into him, revving his libido to an all-time high. Her skin was soft and yielding beneath his hands and he unbuttoned her blouse to feast on her breasts, rewarded by her soft moan.

He'd love to take her right there with old Tony unaware in the other room, but the situation called for a delicate touch. His nails raked the soft inside of her thighs. Oh yeah, she was squirming against him. Her breathing quickened and he slid his hand into the wisp of underwear beneath her skirt. She was wet, hot, and he barely touched her before she shuddered, gasped, and choked back a silent sob of release.

Pleased to have made his point, Sloan stepped back while she straightened her clothes. She gave him a push toward the front room. "You go entertain Tony while I save dinner."

"That won't be nearly as much fun as helping you cook."

"Some help you'd be," she said, buttoning and tucking. "How about setting the dining room table? You do know how to do that, don't you?"

"Your wish is my command."

In the other room, Tony looked up from the computer. "Everything all right in there?"

"You could say," Sloan replied smugly, as he plopped plates and cutlery on the table.

Tony set down the laptop and ambled toward him. "Cassidy explained everything," he said.

"Oh?" Somehow Sloan doubted that.

"Yeah, the fact that you and she used to live next door, but lost track of each other."

"Anything else?"

Tony shrugged. "It's a small town. Lots of old stories about the Hardt brothers breaking hearts." He gave a hesitant laugh.

Sloan clapped him on the back, a little harder than required. "Can't believe those old stories."

"You and your brother had quite the reputations."

"Don't forget about Gramps," Sloan said cheerfully.

"Right," Tony said, clearly out of his depth.

"What is it you do here in West Bend?" Sloan asked.

"I teach at West Bend High."

"I figured it was something like that."

"Dinner!" Cassidy sailed in with a steaming bowl of pasta and Sloan sniffed appreciatively. "Tony, can you grab the salad?"

Sloan took advantage of the fact that her hands were full to fondle her ass as she slid past him to set the dish on the table. She responded by bending over, deliberately shimmying tightly against him. Damn, he wished they were alone; he'd bend her over the table and ease her skirt up and . . .

"Sloan, you can sit here. Tony, over there. Everyone have everything they need?"

Salad and pasta bowls were passed and plates filled. Sloan jumped up and filled everyone's wineglass. He'd barely taken his seat again before he felt the soft, seeking pressure of her bare foot against his leg, playing with the hem of his jeans.

He smiled at her across the table and raised his glass. "I'd like to propose a toast. To West Bend."

Tony chinked his glass with Cassidy. "I'm certainly delighted I wound up here. It's a great place to settle down."

Sloan frowned. Things were not going the way he had planned. "I bet you teach math," he interjected, to break the intimacy between the other two.

"And science." Poor smitten Tony continued to gaze adoringly at Cassidy; little did he know whose foot she was playing with beneath the table.

"Eat up before things get cold, man. Cass and I slaved away in there."

Reluctantly, Tony ripped his attention from Cassidy. "Hard to believe you moved away, with everything West Bend has to offer." His meaning was obvious.

"I had an opportunity I couldn't say no to," Sloan said.

"What kind of opportunity?"

"Ranching. I doubt it would be of much interest to a schoolteacher."

"Or a midwife," Tony said, effectively shutting him down and turning back to Cassidy. "How are things going for Playfair House?"

She shrugged. "It's really still just in the idea stage."

Sloan twirled his pasta, aware that Tony was doing everything in his power to make him feel like the outsider. He'd let the man have his little victory. After all, he'd be the one taking home the spoils.

He nearly choked on his pasta when Cassidy's foot moved up his leg to lodge in that responsive juncture, pressing and burrowing and—

"Yikes! Hot!" he said quickly, taking a sip of wine. He slipped one hand beneath the table, his eyes on Cassidy as he caressed her foot.

Her eyes widened and a secret smile tugged at her lips as she listened to Tony drone on about something. All Sloan could think about was what would happen once he had Cassidy to himself.

He was deep in the middle of a particularly tasty fantasy with strawberries and whipped cream when Tony jumped up and cleared their empty dishes, leaving him alone with Cassidy. Boldly, he thrust against her foot with his crotch. His breathing deepened as he continued to fantasize all that he'd do to her once he got her alone.

"Thanks, Tony." She pulled her foot free and stood up.

Sloan glanced behind him. Yup, good old Tony was back.

"I'm sure you boys will understand that it's been a long day, so I'll say good night now."

Sloan smiled to himself. Clearly she was trying to preserve her reputation. Fair enough. He'd drive away in plain view of the teacher, then double back to the alley behind.

Unfortunately, good old Tony had the same idea.

Cassidy was brushing her teeth when she heard a suspicious thump on the back porch. She switched on the outside light, illuminating Sloan and Tony in fisticuffs like a couple of schoolboys.

"What, might I ask, is going on here?"

"I caught him trying to sneak back inside," Sloan said, wiping blood from his lip.

"Only because I got here first," Tony said. He had a rapidly swelling eye. "What the hell are you doing back here, anyway?"

"None of your damn business."

"Tell him, Cassidy," Tony said. "Which one of us were you playing footsie with during dinner?"

Sloan laughed out loud. "Apparently both of us. What were you up to, Cass? Hedging your bets?"

"The two of you are complete morons," Cassidy blustered, but she blushed furiously and avoided both their gazes.

"Which one of us were you hoping would take you up on the unspoken invitation?" Sloan asked.

"Neither of you. Now get lost. I'm going to bed. Alone!"

In the dark, she listened as both their vehicles started up and drove away. The economical sound of Tony's modest vehicle was drowned out by the heavy growl of Sloan's farm truck, further emphasizing the differences between the men. She lay there, listening in case either of them returned, knowing she should be happy when neither one did.

It had been a silly stunt she'd pulled tonight. But with two men vying for her attention, she'd enjoyed herself fully.

Sloan was proving to be more than a handful. The fact that he'd followed her home sent her into panic mode, and she'd thought it was clever of her to buffer his presence with Tony. Instead, all it had done was reinforce the futility of her situation. Could she really be in love with one man and marry someone else?

Inviting Tony over had been a mistake. Side by side, the differences in the two men were even more marked. Damn Sloan for coming here. She'd heard love could grow between two people who admired and respected each other and chose to make a life together. But she couldn't marry Tony, given the feelings she had for Sloan. She cared for him too much to shortchange him of the grand passion he deserved.

Sloan, on the other hand, was like a wild horse that needed its freedom to thrive and survive. There would be no subduing or domesticating that untamed spirit. It had been wrong of her to try.

She was still tossing and turning when the phone rang.

"Cassidy? Thank God you're back. It's Mike Nemchuck. Julie says it's time."

Cassidy was instantly awake and on her feet. "Where is she now?"

"She's right here, having a bath."

"Can I talk to her, please?"

"Hi, Cassidy. Told you I'd wait till you got back," Julie said.

"I'm glad you did. You doing okay?"

"Like rolling off a log."

"See you soon."

Cassidy grabbed her bag and raced to her car. It was pitch-black on the country road to the Nemchuck's farm and she saw fast-approaching headlights in her rearview mirror. She knew the road like the back of her hand and had no qualms about speeding, but she wished the other driver wouldn't follow so close.

Mile after mile the other vehicle hugged her back bumper and it started to creep her out. Finally she saw her destination up ahead. She turned down the drive, seriously uneasy when the vehicle behind followed suit.

She parked and got out of the car, just as the door of the truck behind her opened, motor still running, headlights revealing its driver.

"Sloan Hardt! You scared the bejesus out of me. Why are you following me in the middle of the night?"

"Is this where Teacher Tony lives?"

"You're interfering in something that doesn't concern you."

He moved to stand between her and the farmhouse. "Wait a sec. Hear me out."

She was so angry, she could barely speak. She pushed at his chest. "Get out of my way. I've got a client inside about to give birth."

The front door of the farmhouse opened, silhouetting the figure of a man. "Hi, Cassidy."

"Coming, Mike," she called, then turned to Sloan in exasperation. "Linda Nemchuck is about to have her sixth child in seven years. She can't tolerate the pill and her husband is too macho to have a vasectomy, even though they're struggling to feed the kids they already have. She's just our age, and she's already old and tired out.

"So if *you're* so damn adamant about not having children, do the right thing." She pushed past him and went up the steps of the farmhouse. "Better yet, help Mike move the kids over to the barn. Linda doesn't want them to hear her giving birth."

Chapter Twelve

Could he possibly be a more selfish bastard?

It was a shock to see Cassidy in her professional life, for he'd only thought of her as an accessory to somehow fit into his life. Not only did she have her own life, there was no room in it for him; and the last thing she needed was his presence, messing things up.

His gut screamed at him to get back in the truck and drive fast and far away, but he ignored it, parked his truck, and followed her into the run-down farmhouse.

She pointed to a narrow staircase. "The kids are upstairs. Go with Mike."

He'd never had much to do with kids and there sure seemed to be a lot of them; wide-eyed and white-faced, some more awake than others, nested together in a dormitory-style bedroom under the eaves. The dad held one that looked too small to walk.

"Do you mind carrying Mac?" Mike asked.

Sloan picked up the second smallest, who took his thumb out of his mouth and pointed to a tattered bear with one ear. Sloan scooped the bear up in his other hand and followed the line of kids and their dad down the steps, conscious of the fragile feel of the skinny body in his arms and the way the youngster pillowed his head trustingly on Sloan's shoulder.

He flinched at the sound of a muffled cry as they passed the parents' bedroom and hoped the youngsters were too sleepy to notice. He brought up the rear of the procession out the front door and down the sagging steps.

Inside the barn, each child picked up a blanket from a stack near the door, then they nested down in a heap of hay. Sloan had only seen animals huddle together for comfort and warmth before. He remained standing, hands stuffed in his pocket, his tiny bundle delivered.

"Thanks, man," Mike said. "I gotta go back in there." He indicated the farmhouse with a sideways motion of his head.

"But—"

"You don't have to stay," Mike said. "They'll be okay. Besides, I shouldn't be too long."

Sloan looked down at all those trusting eyes. "Guess there's no place else I need to be for a while."

He pulled up a stool and watched the kids gradually settle down. They had to know something was up, but were too young to understand what.

"Mister, I gotta pee." It was the little dude named Mac that he'd carried over. The kid stood in front of him in mismatched pajamas, looking defenseless and small.

"Okay. Where?"

Tiny shoulders shrugged. Outside, Sloan figured.

"Let's go then." He rose, trying to make his voice sound authoritative, as if he did this every day. Small, cold fingers slid into his.

The youngster led the way to a shadowy maple tree, its branches silhouetted against a moonlit sky. He stood close, aimed at the tree, and laughed when he hit it.

"Careful of the back splash," Sloan warned.

"Back splash," the little one parroted, seeming delighted with a new word.

Job complete, he scampered back to the barn.

It seemed like Sloan had barely settled back onto his stool when Mike returned and announced it was a girl, clearly torn between staying to reassure the kids and wanting to be with his wife.

Sloan was no good with any of it.

As soon as he could he literally took off, the promise of dawn in the sky as he flew back to Black Creek.

He landed feeling like he'd been away months, rather than a mere week. Was it his imagination or had the landscape changed in his absence? The hills looked blacker and the ranch land greener as the sun rolled over the horizon and woke up the rest of the countryside.

The ranch house was just starting to stir as he headed for Helen's old wing, where he was bunking until his house was finished.

"You're back awful soon." Steele came across him tiptoeing down the hall, boots in hand.

"What are you doing up so early?"

"Heard the plane come in. What happened?"

"Nothing. I just realized she doesn't fit into my world, any more than I fit into hers."

"You gave up, you mean?"

"More like bowed out gracefully."

They faced off and Sloan knew what Steele was thinking: *Hardts aren't quitters.*

"Can't quit something you never start," he said.

Steele slowly nodded and Sloan knew there would be no further discussion if that was his choice.

"How'd *you* do it?" he blurted.

"Do what?"

"Make your life here with Montana?"

"I can live and work anyplace. Black Creek was an easy choice."

"Yeah, but . . ."

"I didn't sacrifice anything to live here. No more than you did when you decided to take over the ranch."

"For Cassidy to live here would never work. This is my life here, not hers."

"You two talk about it?"

No," Sloan said. "And I don't want to talk about it now."

Steele's eyebrows rose. "You brought it up."

"And now I'm dropping it."

One week blurred into another as Sloan worked the ranch and spent every spare second on his house. His goal was to have the house finished by the time Montana had the baby.

Though he had his own private suite, he was sure the new parents would appreciate the place to themselves. He grinned. Besides, he'd heard babies cried all the time.

If he'd hoped the exhausting pace at which he drove himself would erase Cassidy from his mind, it seemed to have the opposite effect. Anytime he was alone, which was often, his thoughts would wander off. Wondering what she was doing. Wondering if she thought about him half as often as he thought about her.

"I am not stepping down from my duties as chamber of commerce president," Montana told Steele in no uncertain terms.

"Fine. If you're so hell-bent on going to that meeting, then I'll drive you," Steele said.

"If you seriously think I'm only leaving the house when you're around to mollycoddle me, you'd better think again."

"The doctor told you to slow down and take these last months easy."

"That old quack! Like he's ever had a baby!"

Montana swung about and stomped away. Smart man that he was, Steele knew better than to follow her.

She felt like she was going stir-crazy, stuck in the house. Steele had already brainwashed the spa staff that she shouldn't be working and if she went over there they treated her like an invalid. The whole situation pissed her off.

Not thinking things through beyond the fact that it felt good to be doing something, anything, she saddled Brown Sugar and hauled herself into the saddle, no easy feat while pregnant.

But it was worth the effort. The horse kept to a leisurely walk, and she felt her agitation melt away. She'd just get a little fresh air, then go back to the house and have a nap like a good girl. She now tired easily, which also irritated her no end, since she'd intended to work till the pains began, squeeze out the baby, and go straight back to work.

Her body was telling her otherwise. So was Steele. *That* was the part she found most irritating.

She was basking in her renewed sense of freedom when her peace was shattered by the angry pounding of hooves coming toward her fast. She looked over her shoulder to see Steele bearing down hard.

"What the hell do you think you're doing, woman?" Brown Sugar had stopped altogether by the time Steele's horse reached them.

"Hi there, yourself." Montana ignored his glower. Steele had become disgustingly overprotective as her pregnancy advanced. While at first she thought it was cute, she'd had enough fussing to last this lifetime and into the next.

"Are you making a career out of defying me?"

"I suggest you quit bossing me around like I'm incapable of thinking for myself." They glared at each other while their horses shifted uneasily, as if aware of the tension.

Tension Sloan sensed from a mile off as he made his way toward them. It was easy to see Steele had pissed Montana off good. Steele was the king of pissing people off and he had an annoying habit of demanding his own way, regardless of the wishes of anyone else.

Sloan straightened and rode into the fray. "How's the mother-to-be? On your way to see how my house is coming along?"

"Don't you dare encourage her!" Steele turned his wrath on Sloan, exactly as Sloan intended.

"Didn't you tell me the doc said she wasn't to get upset or agitated?"

"Stay out of this, Sloan," Steele growled.

He shrugged. "Just taking an interest in my family."

"What's wrong?" Steele suddenly asked. Anger forgotten, he edged closer to Montana, his voice soft and concerned.

"Nothing." She brushed her brow with the back of her hand as color seemed to drain from her face. "Just a little dizzy all of a sudden."

Steele dismounted in a flash and swung himself up behind Montana. He put his arms protectively around her as he gathered the reins and pulled her back against him.

"I've been an insensitive oaf."

She turned her head and rested on him, clearly glad of the support. "Yes, you have," she murmured. "*Your* life hasn't changed in the least. I'm the one who's gotten fat and clumsy."

"You two take the scenic route back," Sloan said. "I'll see

to Rowly." He grabbed the reins to Steele's horse and headed back to the stables. Once back in the ranch house, he called the doctor's office and booked himself an appointment.

Cassidy dropped her purse and keys on the kitchen table and headed for the bathroom, where she turned the taps on full and chucked in a huge handful of bath crystals, hoping they lived up to the label's promise of calming properties. In her bedroom she peeled off her clothes and grabbed a robe, then twisted her hair into a knot on top of her head.

These days, it seemed like each tiny triumph was destined to be followed by a new obstacle with her drop-in mother-and-baby center.

She struggled to pull the cork from the bottle of Viognier she'd bought on the way home, celebrating the fact that her business plan had finally been accepted. West Bend was such a conservative small town in so many ways. Citizens didn't want to admit their teenagers might be having sex and any girls who found themselves in trouble were hustled away, out of sight.

Where once the babies would have been quietly adopted, Cassidy knew the majority of today's young mothers were keeping their infants, only to find themselves totally unprepared for life as a single mom with few resources.

The town council wouldn't budge on rezoning the house she wanted to buy, pressured by the neighbors who didn't want anything to do with a drop-in center in the neighborhood, convinced it would attract undesirable elements and devalue their properties.

She poured a big glass of wine and took it into the bathroom where bubbles mounded above the tub's rim. She lit half a dozen candles, hit the play button on her small stereo, and eased down into the tub's depths.

She rested her head back against the bath pillow and did what she had promised herself she wouldn't; closed her eyes and thought of Sloan, imagining he was here with her. As she sipped her wine she'd be able to talk over her day, with him giving her new ideas and insights. Then he'd take her mind off things in that special way of his.

Her body tingled at the memory of Sloan's hands. Sloan's mouth. Sloan's body.

She should have changed the CD; the singer crooned on about that one special lover she could never have.

Cassidy set down her wine, then slowly started to massage her breasts. Her nipples crested. Pleasurable warmth suffused her, intensifying the demanding throb nesting low in that hidden corridor of pleasure.

She gave a heavy sigh of longing, laced with desire. She mounded bubbles in her palm, scooped them onto her breasts, then gently blew them off, feeling her nipples respond to the soft whisper of her breath.

She viewed herself in the mirror. Candlelight was definitely a girl's best friend. She even liked her hair this way, swept up messily with a riot of curling escaped tendrils. Her face glowed from the heat, dewed with perspiration.

She dragged her nails across her nipples, circled their rosy shape, then scooped her breasts together in her palms as if offering them to her imaginary lover.

Her fingers trailed down across her abdomen and lower, seeking out that chasm that throbbed and pulsed with need. She closed her eyes, immersed in her fantasies as she sought out the stamen in her pleasure lily. The beautiful, sensitive nub rose to attention beneath her fingertip, rewarding her with the first ripples of pleasurable release.

The fantasy felt so real, she didn't want it to end. She imagined Sloan's lips on her neck, Sloan's hands on her breasts heightening the current of pleasure that charged through her bloodstream to her womb, nesting in that secret triangle.

Her breathing quickened in anticipation. An inner surge radiated through her, bringing with it a wave of release so intense she arched up and let out a cry.

She kept her fingers where they were, a soothing weight on that female part of her, absorbing the after-ripples, as the pulsing slowly gentled.

But if her hands were down there, whose hands were on her breasts?

She screamed, then sat up as she batted Sloan's hands away.

"Cassidy, it's okay. It's okay."

"How— How—" She couldn't speak; her heart was racing.

"I thought you saw me in the mirror. I didn't mean to scare you. I called out when I came in, but the music was on. Then I just kind of joined in."

She stared at him in disbelief as the shock slowly faded. He *wasn't* a figment of her imagination. He was very real and virile, and here in her bathroom.

He perched on the edge of the tub and cupped her face, playing with the wisps of hair. "You are so beautiful. I couldn't stay away."

She caught her breath in a tiny gasp of disbelief. How many years had she longed to hear those words, dreamed of this moment where Sloan regarded her with a mixture of longing and need?

When she rose to her feet, he pulled a towel from the heater and wrapped her in it, then lifted her out of the tub and into his arms.

In her room he laid her on the bed, where he unwrapped her as if she was a special gift, feasting his eyes on each revealed inch.

She reached up and tugged at his shirtfront and he pulled it over his head, not bothering with the buttons.

Then he lowered himself atop her, his muscled arms bulging as he supported his weight above her and proceeded to bathe her with his tongue.

Chapter Thirteen

Candlelight filtered in from the bathroom, providing the room's only illumination. The bedroom was cool after the warmth of her bath and she shivered, caught between the contrast of the cool air and the heat of Sloan's mouth.

She swore to always remember him as he looked at this very instant; shirtless, jeans-clad, his hair endearingly messy, his jaw darkened with a day's whisker growth, his eyes darkly intent on her, filled with promise. She framed his face in her hands, still barely able to believe he was real. He turned and pressed a quick, hot kiss to her palm as if to assure her he was. She gave a deep sigh of contentment. There would be plenty of time later to talk.

"Don't move a muscle. Just lie still and enjoy me enjoying you."

She complied as Sloan worshiped every inch of her, discovering erogenous zones she hadn't known existed. No body part was overlooked or unappreciated. He licked and sipped and nibbled, murmuring his approval the entire time as he explored the soft underside of her arms, the bend of her elbow, the back of her knees.

By the time he flicked his tongue across the seam at the top of each leg her entire body was on fire, quivering, tingling, experiencing a need more intense than any before.

It wasn't simply about touch and taste and feel, but so much more.

The Sloan she used to know and the Sloan she knew now merged and blended; the Sloan of her imaginings, the Sloan of her dreams.

She ignored the inner voice that warned her this was no shipboard fling. This was her life, her bed, her being, invaded as surely as Sloan had always invaded her thoughts and her dreams.

At this moment, it was everything she wanted. This moment, with this man.

She felt the erotic abrasion of his whiskers against her soft inner thigh, teasing, torturing, circumventing her needful, throbbing inner sanctum.

Closer to the prize he moved, outlining her inner-lily shape. She could feel the heat of his breath. The slightest shift from her would ensure he hit the target, but she didn't move; couldn't move.

She fought the sense of helplessness and just went with the experience. And as she did, something wonderful happened.

Deep inside her she felt a flood of confidence, a surge of renewal. Sloan hadn't drained her, he'd renewed and recharged her. And as the rush of power raced through her, he nuzzled that delightful inner glory of her womanhood, tongued it, and brought her to the ultimate fulfillment. She swore her entire body lifted off the bed in shuddering ecstasy.

"My God, what did you just do to me?" After-ripples surged through her like live electric currents and she knew nothing would ever be the same.

"Honey, I'm just getting started." He peeled off his jeans and stood before her, a primal male. His magnificent cock jutted forward and her mouth watered at the sight.

He brushed himself against her, following the path his mouth had taken earlier. Her breasts. Her underarm, her belly. Her knees. His cock was like a magic wand, inflaming her almost to the breaking point as he nuzzled her labia and teased her clit, moving back when she attempted to arch toward him, to make him hers.

"I want you!" It came out an imperial demand.

He laughed. "Do you always get what you want?"

"Hardly ever."

"Then let's make this the exception."

He rolled onto his back and pulled her with him so she straddled him.

She rubbed her heated mons against him, resisting the temptation to fling herself upon him, to pleasure-ride the joystick that stood at the ready. "My turn to tease you."

She slid herself across him, legs wide, feeling the pleasurable tingles radiating through her sensitized clit as it hugged the contours of his torso. She rubbed back and forth, the moisture of her own power and excitement dampening his skin. She leaned forward and dragged her breasts across his face, avoiding his seeking mouth.

Finally she let him tug her breasts in his mouth, sucking one while tweaking the other, trading back and forth.

Panting and writhing, she took his cock in her hand and angled it to her clit, used it like a love toy to stimulate herself to orgasm. She came with a tiny sob, then fisted his cock and pumped it against her, her damp hand alternately stimulating him and her until, with a triumphant cry, she took him. Her insides gloved him with moist heat, muscles clenching and releasing as she embraced him from the inside.

Hands on his chest for balance, she rode him shamelessly, bucking and arching, moving back and forth and side to side in a frenzy. His hands grasped her hips to slow her down, but she evaded his efforts and redoubled hers, the force of her orgasm hurtling him after her into the great abyss.

Thoroughly spent, she collapsed atop him. It seemed a long time before either of them mustered up the energy to speak. Who needed words after what they'd just shared?

"Tell me you're really here," she said, smoothing the sweat-dampened planes of his torso. "That I didn't just conjure you up from my imagination."

He pushed her hair back off her forehead in a loving, intimate way, as if he felt he needed to see all of her. "I'm here." He tugged the sheet up to cover them as they lay together, limbs entangled, breathing gradually returning to normal.

She hadn't known how much she'd craved his touch. Even now, sated, she couldn't stop fondling him, as if her touch had the power to keep him with her.

"It was a spontaneous decision."

"I adore spontaneity."

"I even brought your favorite crispy ginger beef and broccoli."

"You brought food? What are you waiting for? Bring it on!"

"I knew I couldn't impress you with my own cooking."

She caught his hand as he started to get up. "Why do you feel you need to impress me at all?"

" 'Impress' is probably a bad choice of words."

He returned with two cartons of takeout and chopsticks and sat alongside her. Cassidy melted. Chinese food in bed with Sloan; another dream come true. Suddenly she was ravenous and the disappointments of her day evaporated in the afterglow of utter contentment.

"I don't think life gets any better than this."

Sloan cleared his throat as if suddenly uncomfortable. He turned, put down his food, and faced her.

"I have something to ask you. You don't have to answer right away. Take your time."

Omigod! She'd never dared imagine he'd propose!

"Okay." She swallowed her sudden rush of excitement, keeping her gaze and her voice even.

"Would you consider coming and staying at Black Creek till after Montana has the baby?"

"What?" She stiffened and clutched the sheet to her breasts, as if it could protect her from what she'd just heard.

"It's asking a lot, I know. But I've never seen Steele so freaked. Montana's been restricted to bed rest and she's not taking it well. The ranch is so far from town, if anything should happen to her or the baby . . ."

Cassidy felt as if her insides had been ripped out. Sloan wasn't here because of her. He was here because of his family.

Why had she even let herself dream? Why had she wasted her energy?

"I have other clients," she said flatly.

"I understand," Sloan said. "But you also have a partner. Surely she could handle things for a short time while you're away, like she did while you were on the cruise."

He'd been checking on her. She wasn't sure if she ought to be flattered or offended. "Why is Montana on bed rest?"

"Her blood pressure's high."

"How high?"

Sloan gave a shrug.

"Hypertension is not uncommon with a first pregnancy."

"She's taking it awful personally; like she did something wrong, somehow failed at being pregnant."

"That's hardly going to help."

Sloan reached for her hand. "It's a mess there right now.

Steele's falling apart. If you were there, I know everyone would be more easy."

"And you get to save the day. The hero shows up, midwife in tow, just in the nick of time."

"This isn't about me, Cass."

"Of course it is, Sloan. It always was."

"Will you at least think about it?"

"I don't need to think about it. I'll do it."

"You will?"

"Of course. It's what I do."

"That's great!" Sloan got out of bed and started to dress.

Before she could even ask him what he was doing, the phone rang in the other room and she hurried to answer it. Better to distance herself from Sloan anyway.

"Hey, beautiful."

"Hi, Tony." She sank into a chair, thinking with relief how uncomplicated he was. So unlike Sloan.

"I just heard the bad news. I wanted to say I'm sorry, but don't give up. It's only the first stab at it."

"I know. I have no intention of going down without a fight." She twisted a strand of hair around her finger. Good, constant, reliable Tony. Why couldn't she love him?

"That's my girl. Is there anything I can do?"

"I can't think of anything right now. I'll let you know if I do."

"I was thinking along the lines of coming over and rubbing your back."

She gave a quick, nervous laugh. "Actually, I'm already in bed. Rain check?"

"Of course. I've got a call in to a couple of buddies from college. One's a lawyer, one's a politician. If anyone can help us figure how to get some forward motion, it's these guys."

"Tony, you don't have to do that. This is my fight."

"I'd do anything for you, Cass. You know that."

"I do. And I really appreciate your support."

"Sweet dreams, then. I'll call you tomorrow."

"Okay."

Only after she'd hung up did she become aware of Sloan lounging against the door frame as if he belonged there.

"Who are you fighting with?"

Sloan had a pretty good idea of who'd called and he didn't like the way it made him feel. Or was it that it made him feel at all? The fact that Tony knew stuff, shared things with Cassidy. . . . He didn't like the feeling of exclusion that gave him. Damn good thing he was getting her away from Mr. Goody Two-shoes.

"You know the old expression, you can't fight city hall? Well, I am."

She tried to move past him, but he stayed his ground. "Tell me more."

Short of pushing him out of the way, she had no choice but to fill him in. "I want to open a drop-in resource center for young moms and their babies. And I have no intention of letting a bunch of stuffy politicians and their fear of voter reaction stop my goals."

"Where are you with this project?"

He saw her shoulders slump beneath the thin silk of her short robe. "I'm tired. It's been a long day."

"But something happened today. Share it with me."

"There's nothing you can do."

"Sure there is." He reached for her and pulled her close. "Lean on me. Let me take some of it off your shoulders. Believe it or not, Cass, I'm a really good listener."

He felt her soften, relax against him. Maybe it wasn't so tough doing this understanding male stuff, after all. Something he'd never had the urge to do before now.

They sat down together, her curled on his lap as she told him about her plans for Playfair House and the property she'd found that would be so perfect, except for the snag with the zoning.

He listened, inserting an occasional comment but mostly just holding her, touched by her dedication and insight.

After a while, though, he started to feel overwhelmed. Maybe he wasn't strong enough to share her burdens. Maybe he wasn't the guy he thought he was. All he knew was that he had to get out of there, before it was too late.

It was almost as if she sensed him stepping back emotionally, because she did the same, untangling herself physically from him.

"When do you want to leave for Black Creek?"

"How about if I come by for you first thing in the morning?"

He was leaving now?

Of course he was. Here one minute, gone the next. That was Sloan. On the ship, he'd made it clear that he didn't want to spend the night with her. Why would that be any different now?

"Do Steele and Montana know you're here?"

Sloan shook his head. "I wasn't sure you'd agree and I didn't want to raise everyone's hopes."

"Smart idea," she said dryly.

After Sloan left, Cassidy made herself a cup of tea. While it steeped, she turned on her computer to check her e-mail.

There was correspondence from one of the council members with some ideas on how she might go about getting the project approved. The unexpected help lifted her mood.

She shut off the computer and went to close the blinds when she noticed a vehicle in the back alley. No one should be parked out there! She put on her boots and jacket and grabbed a flashlight.

The sky was perfectly clear, alive with the jewel-like wink of hundreds of stars and a tiny sliver of moon as she approached the shadowy pickup, expecting amorous teens. When she flashed the light through the driver's window, a figure stirred and straightened just as she wrenched open the driver's door.

"Sloan Hardt, what on earth are you doing out here?"

"Thought I'd catch a few winks before morning."

"I thought you were going out to the farm?"

"I didn't want to worry Gramps and your mom. I figured it was better if they thought I came to be with you."

"But you acted like you didn't want to stay," she said, confused.

He caught her hand and linked their fingers. "Cass, I didn't want to assume that I could drop in and spend the night with you anytime the urge grabbed me. You have a life."

They stared at each other, so near and yet so far. Finally she heaved a heavy sigh.

"You'd better come in. Otherwise, the neighbors will really start to wonder."

She turned and stomped back to the house. She was almost to the porch before she heard the slam of the truck's door and the sound of Sloan behind her.

"I thought I was being a gentleman. Why are you so mad?"

"Shut up, Sloan." Inside, she rooted through a chest, then tossed him pillows and a blanket. "The couch pulls out. I'll see you in the morning." Then she marched into her bedroom and shut the door very firmly.

Sloan rolled over and punched the pillow. The couch was only marginally more comfortable than the truck. Why did he have the feeling he'd totally said and done the wrong thing?

He'd had no intention of sleeping with her again. But when he'd seen her in the tub, so sexy and sexual. . . .

He was *almost* ashamed to admit how happy he was to be getting her away from Tony. He had no business to feel that way; to feel so possessive toward Cassidy.

He flashed on the sudden image of her in bed, sleep-tousled and relaxed, and got aroused all over again. It was a sight he could easily see himself anticipating every morning.

No, too scary. He wasn't the settling-down type. He'd

avoided spending the night with her on the ship because he knew how damn hard it would be to pull himself away from her in the morning.

It should be easier out at Black Creek; the ranch was big enough that he could put as much distance between them as he wanted.

Chapter Fourteen

It turned out that the damned ranch wasn't nearly big enough, although Cassidy proved a welcome addition. Not only did she calm Steele down while keeping a watchful eye on Montana, everyone on the entire ranch seemed to breathe a little easier as the tension dissipated.

Sloan cleared out of Helen's wing and moved into the bunkhouse, which was still too close. He'd taken to working late into the evening on his own place, often staying out there for the night, a safer distance from the ranch house and Cassidy.

Which only made it more unexpected to see her jouncing up the rutted dirt driveway in an open ranch Jeep, sunlight gleaming off her red-gold hair.

She stepped out of the Jeep and turned her attention to his house, inspecting the bones of his personal design. He thought he detected an approving nod before she picked her way up the makeshift front steps and over a pile of freshly swept sawdust to reach him.

She cocked her head and studied him, unabashed. "There is definitely something about a man in a tool belt that screams testosterone."

Sloan's breath whistled from between his teeth. She eyed him as if he was naked beneath the tool belt; a total turn-on. He shifted uncomfortably from foot to foot while she glanced around in interest.

"So this is the dream house? Do I get a tour?"

"Sure. How's the mother-to-be?"

"Fed up by the entire process. In other words, perfectly normal." Cassidy laughed. "I thought it would be good for her and Steele to have some time alone together." She held up a brown bag and a Thermos. "I brought coffee and fresh cinnamon buns."

"Keep that up and the tool belt will need to be let out."

"I've been worried about you suffering on bunkhouse cooking. I came to invite you for dinner tonight."

"What's the occasion?"

"Steele and I are taking Montana to town tomorrow for some tests. I fully expect them to admit her and induce labor, so it'll be the last family dinner for a while."

"Isn't it too soon?"

"She's close to term and the baby is a good size. There's protein in her urine, so the placenta's breaking down, which means it's time to get the show on the road." She looked down, then directly at him. "You didn't have to move out, you know."

"No matter," Sloan said shortly. "I'm comfortable enough in the bunkhouse."

"Which must be why you're spending most nights out here."

"You keeping tabs on me, Cass?"

She continued to meet his gaze squarely. "What if I am?"

Disconcerted, he looked past her and ran a hand through his hair. "I'm a selfish bastard. I can't deny it suits me to have you here."

"You'd never know it, by the way you're keeping your distance."

"It's for the best. We both know I can't give you what you want."

"How do you even know what I want?"

Sloan cleared his throat. "I'm booked for a vasectomy next week."

"Then I've got a good few days to have my way with you."

"Don't, Cass." Damn, but he wanted to hold her. To be the one to give her those babies she hankered after.

"Sloan, I'm teasing." But neither of them was laughing. "It's your decision. You have to do what feels right for you."

"I can't give you the picket fence and rug rats you want."

"I know that."

"You deserve more than an hour here and an hour there. And sooner or later you'd resent me for that."

"I know that, too." She took a step closer. "Still, I can't help but remember. . . ."

"Remember what?"

"That night in the barn. We were hiding from my father, remember? And you promised you'd always be there for me."

He nodded, took her hand in his, and traced the tiny white scar on her pinkie. "We pricked our fingers and swore an oath."

Her hand trembled slightly in his. "You do remember."

He cupped her face in his hand. "Some things are pretty damn tough to forget."

She pressed his hand to her cheek. "Some things are just too big."

Sloan moved back a step and ignored how cold his hand felt without hers against it. "Tony's the guy for you. He'll give you everything you want."

"I'm not looking for a man to fix my life, Sloan. I want one who enhances my life."

He turned away. "Come on. I'll show you around the place." She'd see soon enough that it was bachelor digs. No family room, no nursery, no fancy walk-in closet with room for dozens of pairs of sexy shoes.

He'd designed it spare and lean, with an open floor plan

that encouraged the indoors to flow to the outside. He'd spent a fortune on windows that he had no intention of covering with drapes. He loved the view, the hills, the river. Underfoot were sturdy wood floors, a place a man could walk through wearing his boots. And ignore the empty sound of only one set of footfalls.

"You can see big sky country from every room," she said as she followed him through a space that suddenly seemed mocking in its emptiness.

She was the first person who got it, who understood his design. Cassidy always had a way of seeing inside him like no one else; that's probably what sent him running.

Which meant he wasn't selfish, but a coward.

He loved her and he was going to turn her over to another man, because he loved her that much. And it was something he'd never be able to explain, not to himself, not to her, not to anyone.

"Nice kitchen," she said teasingly. "Are you going to learn how to cook?"

"Don't, Cass."

"What? Remind you that you're not perfect?"

"Perfect? I'm the most flawed human being I know."

"If that's what you think, you should get out more." Her eyes flirted with his, weighted by an emotion he didn't want to see.

"*You* should get out more." He gave her arm a playful swat. "What about those cinnamon buns I was promised?"

"First I want to see your bedroom." There was intimacy

in those words and part of him screamed out to run, to escape. But he couldn't.

"It's this way."

The bedroom was a generous size, with a high sloping ceiling, floor-to-ceiling windows that framed the view, and glass doors to the wraparound deck.

He'd built the bed himself, rough-hewn logs he'd cut down, peeled, and cured, then lightly sanded to retain the unique texture of each post. He'd finished it off with a huge wooden slab of a headboard.

His gut clenched when she ran a hand lovingly over the wood, almost as if she touched him.

"You made this."

"It was a pain in the ass to move," he said. "It weighs a ton. Had to take it apart and put it back together."

"It's perfect here. You must have had this bed in mind when you designed the house."

"I must be the one man crazy enough to design a house to match his bed."

"You mean to match *you*."

When had she moved so close? Or had he come to her? Somehow it didn't matter.

He looked from Cassidy to the bed, then back to her. How had he not understood that he'd had her in mind when he built it? He'd seen her there in his dreams, her red-gold hair fanned across the pillow. To this day he'd never taken a woman to that bed, knowing subconsciously it would be wrong.

He cleared his throat thickly. "Let's go get that coffee."

She continued to gaze at him knowingly and he felt split open like a watermelon.

"Yes, let's," she said.

They took their coffee and cinnamon buns out onto the deck where Sloan brushed off the one Adirondack chair and insisted she take it.

"You're not quite set up for company yet, are you?"

He rested one booted foot on the arm of her chair and leaned on his bent knee, staring thoughtfully around him. "I don't know if I ever will be. I like the idea of keeping it a safe haven."

"Funny, I never thought of you as a loner. At school you were always in a pack."

"I work with people all day. It'll be nice to come home to peace and quiet."

"I guess taking on Black Creek is quite a change from running James's spread."

He finished his coffee and tossed the dregs over the side. "I was ready for a change."

"It means a lot, having a place that's truly yours. I remember when I first bought my place."

Why were the gods torturing him this way? Tossing in his face the one and only woman who would ever truly know him; the one whose soul touched his? Was he being punished for all those years of sowing wild oats? For taking, then discarding the female affections that came his way?

Cassidy wasn't sure what was going on or what had happened to Sloan's cocky self-assurance. The boy-who'd-had-it-all had matured into the man-who-had-it-all, and that's who she'd met onboard the ship. The Sloan who'd slept in his truck outside her house rather than make assumptions of his welcome; that was someone else. Had she done that to him?

In her quest to teach him a lesson, had she stripped his confident veneer, or was she giving herself too much credit? Maybe this was the real Sloan, hardworking, serious, and solo, and she'd just never seen him for who he really was, preferring her fantasy version.

As long as she kept him her "fantasy man" she knew he wasn't real, so she couldn't have him. It made the loss somehow bearable. For she knew, in her heart of hearts, this was one situation where they both wound up losing.

He stood so close, seeming to read her thoughts. In what felt like the most natural move in the world, she stood, looped her arms around his neck, nuzzled against him, and said, "Take me to bed."

His hands slid from her shoulders to her hips and back to her shoulders, lingering at her waist. She tightened her hold, afraid he was about to reject her.

"There's never been a woman in that bed."

She kept her words light. "So I'll be the first." *Though I want to be the last.*

The bed welcomed her like an old friend when she dropped onto it and waited for him to join her. Sloan reached forward and tugged off her boots. They hit the wood floor with a satisfying thud, followed by his.

He stretched out next to her and played with her hair.

"I've seen you here a hundred times in my dreams. I just didn't realize it was you."

"I think I sensed that." She busied her fingers on the buttons of his shirt, seeking the warm, taut skin beneath. She cupped the front of his jeans where he was hard, growing harder as she fumbled with the zipper.

I love you, Sloan, she thought, hugging the words to her heart.

He unfastened her shirt, unhooked the front of her bra, and reverently touched her breasts, shaping and reshaping them, playing and teasing in a way that was far more arousing than if he'd grabbed at her.

He licked them, his tongue hot, then blew on them, his breath cool. Just the contrast of his work-roughened, sun-darkened hands against the soft white of her flesh was a turn-on. She dragged her palm across his jaw, loving the tingles that traveled up her arm from the contact.

He tugged one nipple into his mouth and rolled it into a ball of sensation she felt deep in her womanhood. Suddenly her jeans were far too constricting. She rolled free, skinned down her jeans and kicked them aside, then tackled his.

The instant she unzipped them his erect cock sprang free. She touched him, marveling at the feel. How could something be both so hard and so soft at the same time? And so many different skin tones, from softest pink to deep red undertoned with mauve. She knelt above him, conscious of the growing damp warmth between her legs. When a shiny drop on the tip of his erection signaled his own arousal, she whisked it away with her tongue, enjoying the salt-sweet contrast, enjoying even more his sigh of pleasure as she circled the entire velvety tip with her tongue, then closed her lips around his girth.

He moaned, encouraging her to continue.

She moved her mouth up and down while lashing her tongue in circles, sucking, then licking, then sucking again.

She hooked his jeans with her bare foot and pushed them down so he could kick them off.

She delved lower, palmed his balls and swirled them with her tongue while she pumped him, firm but slow.

"God, Cass. God, don't!"

She heard him suck his breath through his teeth and knew he was close. Reluctantly she ceased her attentions. Fun as it might be to make him lose control, there were other, far more fun pursuits to undertake.

He slid down her and, too impatient to remove her thong panties, pushed them aside and plundered her needy sweetness.

He used his hands to separate the damp folds guarding her secrets, running a teasing finger from her front crease to the back. He gave a murmur of satisfaction at her hungry sigh.

With perfect precision his tongue honed in on the prize, darting in and out of her entranceway. The damp heat of his mouth enhanced her dew. Lips on lips, he laved and loved, finally lavishing full attention on that quivering, pulsing center, encouraging the pleasure pearl to swell and grow until her entire body arched, trembled, and gave up the response he sought.

Cassidy stuffed her fist in her mouth to muffle her cry as she felt the initial ground swell. When the full impact hit, she grabbed onto the headboard for support.

Instead of giving her time to recover, Sloan began on round two.

Chapter Fifteen

This time she didn't bother trying to muffle anything, not enthusiastic murmurs or frantic pants as she matched his movements with a frenzy all her own. When wave two and wave three hit she was ready and eager for more, sobbing out her pleasure.

The tremors had yet to subside before she turned her back toward Sloan and slid down to his eager readiness.

She'd had her release; time now to torture him. She slid his cock up and down her trembling inner lips, almost but not quite hooking the opening. She heard his groan of frustration, felt him throb impatiently in her palm as she guided him back, pretending to miss the entranceway.

"Cass!"

"Um-hmm." She crowned his tip with her damp palm before she pivoted her hand, enjoying her power. He responded by lightly stroking her backside, tickling the dividing crease, smoothing the curve of her hips.

Her inner muscles clenched, anticipating his possession as she shimmied forward to try him on for size.

Slowly she lowered herself on his pulsing length, muscles tight, enhancing the pleasure for both of them. She felt him surge forward and fill her, as desperate for their joining as she was.

Smoothly their bodies began the dance of love with a pleasure-inducing rhythm that suited them both.

Her snugness sheathed his length to perfection. She was full of him, full with him, filled by him.

She stroked his inner thigh, fondled the tight sack housing his balls, then leaned forward to explore a new angle of entry as he thrust, sliding smoothly in and out and back in.

"Turn around," he said. "I want to watch you come."

"Are you sure?" She did a quick thrust of her own.

He grabbed her and held her in place for a long moment, during which she felt him throbbing within, fighting for control.

"Okay. Now," he said finally.

She eased herself off him, feeling the instant emptiness before she straddled him and slowly took him back inside, inch by loving inch.

"Like that?"

He stared intensely up at her. "Just like that."

"Now what?"

He licked his middle finger and applied the slightest pressure to her clit. "Ready whenever you are."

She rocked back and forth, feeling the pressure of another orgasm. An instant flood this time, wave followed wave of intense pleasure, till his orgasm funneled into hers and together they created one massive surge of unstoppable power.

The transition back to normalcy this time was unusually difficult. The getting up. The fumbling for clothes. Neither mentioned that this would be their last time together. Montana would have her baby and Cassidy would return to West Bend. She cast a final look at that magnificent bed, wondering if he would ever look at it quite the same way again.

Sloan walked her out to the Jeep. "What time's dinner?"

"Anytime after six."

"See you then." He ducked his head in for a quick kiss, just enough that she could taste the way her flavor lingered on his lips.

It was her own fault, Cassidy told herself as she drove back to the ranch house, her vision obscured by tears.

Worse, it was impossible to hide what had just happened from Montana. Damn pregnant women and their extraordinary intuitive powers. Steele bolted at her arrival with a mumbled "be right back," and Montana was obviously eager for the distraction of someone else's life.

"I take it you found Sloan . . . to your satisfaction?"

Cassidy busied herself strapping the blood pressure cuff on Montana's upper arm.

"Come on, Cass, spill. I need to live vicariously through someone."

Cassidy played deaf as she put on the stethoscope. "Don't talk. It'll make your blood pressure go up."

Montana stayed blessedly silent while Cassidy read the numbers. "Well?"

"Same," Cassidy said, removing the cuff and folding it neatly.

"That's not what I meant and you know it."

"I got the grand tour. That's quite the bachelor pad he's building."

Montana snorted with amusement. "Subtle as a hammer, isn't he? It could use some female input."

"I don't think that's on the blueprint."

"He's a lot like Steele, you know—even though he's spent his entire life pretending not to be."

"I know."

"Those Hardt boys need the softening of a woman's influence. Angel agrees with me one hundred percent."

"You'll be happy to hear he's coming for dinner tonight."

"Why don't you seem very happy about that?"

Cassidy bustled around, straightening bedding and plumping pillows. "It doesn't matter to me one way or the other."

Mercifully, Montana changed the subject. "You know what I'm dying for, once I've had this baby?"

Cassidy thought back to her many clients over the years. "A cup of coffee or a glass of wine?"

"Those would both be good, but what I want more is a nice long, soothing soak in the hot tub."

They were interrupted by a knock on the door. "That'll be the massage therapist," Cassidy said.

She helped Montana into position, supported on her side with strategically placed pillows, then excused herself while Willow, one of the spa's therapists, worked her magic.

Back in her guest suite, she checked her e-mails. Things were quiet in West Bend; her partner was holding down the fort nicely. No rush to get back.

Could it be she'd outgrown West Bend? Her mother was happily settled on the ranch with James. Tony would either hang around waiting to wear her down or eventually give up and take a teaching job in a different town. Did she really want to become the town spinster, delivering everyone else's babies?

She should have never revisited her feelings for Sloan. If she hadn't, maybe she would be able to settle for safe, dull Tony and life in West Bend; even convince herself that she was happy.

As she sat staring at the computer she received another e-mail, this time with a photo attached. She opened the message first and read:

> Dear Cassidy,
> I hope this note finds you well. I'm writing to invite you to my graduation ceremony on June 10th.

> That's right, I made it! Whew! You were so right, so encouraging at a time when I really didn't know which way was up. I'm attaching a pic of Joshua. Can you believe he's three already? The main man in his proud momma's life. I'm not sure what would have happened if I hadn't met you when I did, but I doubt I'd be strutting in my cap and gown with a beautiful three-year-old in my arms. Please come. Love you!
>
> Melody

Cassidy swallowed a lump in her throat as she studied the picture. Melody had been a firecracker, rebellious, determined, and scared. Cassidy had found her a family to nanny for, before and after she had her baby. She knew it was the stability of that environment that had helped Melody get back on her feet and complete her education. There were many more like Melody who could benefit from a hand-up, if they only had the resources. That was the reason she had imagined a young mom's resource center in the first place.

On the heels of the idea had come the name. Playfair House would be a safe, home-style environment where moms could support one another, child-mind for one another, improve their life skills, and become better parents. There would be an area of free stuff for exchange, outgrown baby outfits, maternity clothes, household items.

Was it really a pie-in-the-sky dream?

Not if she had her way!

She was turning off the computer when a new thought

struck her. Could it be she'd wanted to have children simply to prove her father wrong? Maybe this alternate way was her pathway. There were hundreds of young Melodys in need of the supportive environment she could provide. Maybe traditional motherhood was not her destiny. It certainly didn't have to be her only one.

Montana was clearly looking forward to their "dinner party" after so many meals in bed.

"Am I the only one who's excited?" she demanded as Cassidy helped her wash and dry her hair. "You came back with that euphoric afterglow that only comes from over-the-top great sex; now you're moping around like your dog got run over."

"Just a few stuffed-shirt bureaucrats I'd happily see run over," Cassidy said.

"Do tell!"

In the face of Montana's enthusiasm, Cassidy found herself telling the other woman about her e-mail from Melody; the frustration and stalls of the process to start up Playfair House.

Montana jumped all over the idea, encouraging Cassidy to go for her dream, sharing some of the headaches and roadblocks she had run into starting up the spa.

"In the end, it's worth all the bullshit to sit back and say to yourself, 'Look what I did.' And it doesn't matter if anyone else sees or appreciates it, just you."

"I'll bear that in mind," Cassidy said as she brushed Montana's hair.

"Any reason your dream location needs to be West Bend?" Montana asked.

"Comfort zone for me, more than anything. That's the area I know, where my reputation is. Why? What are you thinking?"

"Just thinking out loud."

Cassidy finished brushing Montana's hair and loosely braided it, then tied it with a velvet ribbon. "I guess I could consider a different location. One without the uptight attitude of West Bend."

The courtyard patio had been transformed into an outdoor dining room, lit with candles and torches.

A subdued jazz saxophone curled from hidden speakers and added to the sweet scent of fragrant jasmine and other blooms.

The spa staff had gone all out, with tables and chairs draped in gauzy fabric and colorful china and napkins adorning the table.

The Black Creek Spa staff really did love Montana. The chef had shown up personally on his day off to make sure the meal was utter perfection. And even though summer hadn't yet officially arrived, it was giving a good preview, the golden sun dipping low, bathing Black Creek in balmy evening air.

Cassidy thought she was the first to arrive until a human shadow moved into the light. Sloan! Her pulse raced at the sight of him. He was close enough to touch, yet forever out of reach.

"You look very nice," he said.

"Thank you." It had been nice to have a reason to wear her white eyelet flouncy skirt and top. "You look tired," she said.

"I haven't been sleeping all that great." Their strained exchange was interrupted by the arrival of Montana and Steele.

Montana wore a simple black gown, softly flowing from shoulder to ankle, enhancing her rounded shape. Steele held her arm as if she was the most delicate thing on the planet. Even pregnant, she moved with a grace that spoke of her earlier career as a dancer.

She looked around her in delight. "I've been looking forward to this all day. I'm so tired of those four bedroom walls."

Steele filled a wineglass with sparkling water for her, champagne for the rest of them.

"I'd like to propose a toast," he said. "To family and friends, always being there for each other."

"Hear, hear," Montana said. "To Sloan for convincing Cassidy to be here with me, and to Cassidy for neglecting her other clients for me."

"I wouldn't have it any other way." Cassidy took a sip of her wine and washed away a faint twinge of envy, wondering if she would ever feel as serene and settled as Montana did; secure in her environment and basking in all she had accomplished.

Was she forever destined to feel this niggling discontent, that nothing she did, nothing she achieved, was quite good enough?

Their meal was delicious, but she noticed Montana barely

touched a thing on her plate as the Hardt brothers discussed the ranch.

After the meal was ended and the table cleared, Montana entreated Steele to dance with her, which left Cassidy and Sloan sitting awkwardly across from each other.

Cassidy wished she could tell Sloan about her e-mail from Melody, about her frustration with Playfair House, but why would he care about anything in her world?

Sloan cleared his throat. "Steele meant what he said earlier. We all appreciate you being here."

"I know that," Cassidy said. "I'm glad to be able to do it."

"Would you look at that! The second we old folks turn our backs, you youngsters are partying up a storm," a new voice said.

Cassidy turned to see a tanned and smiling older couple. Sloan ambled to his feet and shook their hands.

"Helen! Zeb!" Montana greeted her former mother-in-law and Helen's new husband with a warm hug. "When did you get back? Why didn't you call and let us know you were coming?"

"We wanted to surprise you. I'm just glad we made it back before that grandbaby of mine puts in an appearance."

"Which shouldn't be too long now, according to my midwife here."

Cassidy found herself pulled into the conversation, with introductions all around. Now she really felt out of place, since it was Helen's suite she was occupying.

She pulled back a step, conscious of the love and familiarity flowing between the others.

More chairs were fetched, more toasts drunk and, as darkness fell, a tripod screen was set up at one end of the courtyard while Zeb fiddled with a laptop computer. Moments later the screen was filled with pictures from his and Helen's year-long honeymoon. One that appeared would never end, judging from the way the older couple sat close, gazing at each other with love and touching at every opportunity.

Montana sat holding Steele's hand, glowing with happiness. If only it was contagious.

Helen and Zeb chatted animatedly, narrating some of their antics and finishing each other's sentences in a way that was endearing, till the screen went blank. "There's lots more, of course," Helen said. "But that was enough for now. What have we missed? How's the spa?"

"We have a great line of new products I know you'd love. They're especially beneficial for after the sun." Montana caught Cassidy's eye. "Cass, the spa's still open. Would you mind getting some of that special after-sun cream for Helen to try?"

Cassidy pushed her chair back so fast it almost fell over. "Not at all." She was relieved to have an excuse to get out of the "happy zone"; it was painful to observe something she would never have.

She fetched the cream from the spa and took her time returning. The longer she stayed at Black Creek, the more attached to the place she became. It was such an incredible spot, set under the watchful shadow of the hills, the creek winding through the property.

She loved this time of day, when daylight softened into

dusk. As the light faded, other senses seemed heightened. Her skin became more sensitive to the whisper of air across her bare arms and shoulders and the air was thick with fragrances.

A glider near the house beckoned to her and she settled herself in and pushed against the ground with her foot, setting it in motion.

It was okay being alone. Really it was. She'd always been alone. Except for those times in her childhood when Sloan was with her.

No sooner had Sloan invaded her thoughts than he materialized in person and plunked himself down next to her, upsetting the rhythm of her swing, the rhythm of her life.

"What's the matter?" he asked.

"Why would anything be the matter?"

He made a scoffing sound. "It's me, remember? I was watching you earlier before you headed over here. I could see you getting more and more withdrawn as the evening wore on."

She didn't even bother to deny it. "Everyone here is family. Everyone belongs here except me."

"Cass—"

"Never mind. The more things change, the more they stay the same." She started to rise, but he stopped her with a hand on her arm.

"Can we talk about this?"

"There's nothing to talk about."

"What's going on? Everyone seems so damn emotional right now."

"Everyone except you, Sloan. If you can't manage happy-go-lucky, you're stuck. It's the only feeling you acknowledge."

"That's hardly fair."

"I don't have to be fair."

He pulled her to him. "I'm as confused as you are right now, Cass, feeling equally out of step with things."

Cassidy stiffened. *Don't do it. Hold your ground. He knows you. He knows all your vulnerabilities.*

He was going to kiss her. She steeled herself to resist, to not reach out for what it looked like he was offering, when he had nothing to offer. But at that second his cell phone rang.

"Hardt. Yeah." Abruptly he stood and pulled her with him. "Come on. That was Steele. Something's going on with Montana."

Chapter Sixteen

Cassidy raced back to the others, Sloan at her heels.

"Do you think she's in labor?" he asked.

"I won't know until I examine her," Cassidy said.

"I'm not finished with what we were talking about," Sloan said stubbornly.

But I am. "Sloan, you brought me here to do a job. So let me do it."

Montana, sitting stiffly in her chair as if she was afraid to move, brightened at the sight of Cassidy. Everyone else hovered, uncharacteristically silent.

"Guess what?" Montana said with forced animation as

she stood. She pulled at the front of her dress. "I'd say my water broke."

"It certainly looks that way. Let's get you inside," Cassidy said in her most matter-of-fact tone.

Steele rose, as well. This is where she always felt sorry for the men, particularly those who were used to taking charge. She gave his arm an encouraging pat. "Why don't you stay with the others for now? Montana and I need a little time."

Steele sat back down like a robot, looking shell-shocked. Helen, bless her heart, picked up the conversational ball and the strained air dissipated as Cassidy hustled Montana into her bedroom and checked her over.

"I guess this is it then?" Montana gripped Cassidy's arm hard and Cassidy got that same rush she always did, being in her element.

It wasn't about control, for she had no control over what happened next. What she had were the skills and expertise to orchestrate things to a happy conclusion.

"There's no turning back," Cassidy agreed as she helped Montana into a loose T-shirt of Steele's that she had elected to wear for the birth.

"Is she okay?" Steele hovered anxiously in the background, a typical father-to-be.

"Don't talk about me like I'm not here," Montana said sharply.

He took a breath and approached the bed. "What would you like me to do?"

"Come here. Just be with me." When Montana stretched

out her hand, Steele perched on the bed next to her and gently took her hand in his.

"Does it hurt?"

"Not yet. I'll be sure and let you know."

Steele looked up at Cassidy. "Should we go to the hospital? Just in case?"

"Don't be silly," Montana said. "Cassidy has delivered more babies than the doctor. Besides, what can they do at the hospital that she can't do right here, except try to pump me full of drugs I don't want? Steele, be a love and put on that meditation CD for me, would you?"

After ensuring Montana was comfortable, Cassidy went to reassure the others, but there was no reassuring Sloan.

"I want to talk to you. Alone!"

She didn't appreciate the way Sloan glowered at her. "I'm busy."

"I can see that you're busy. Busy engineering this!"

She laughed. "I can hardly control when a woman goes into labor."

"You knew that having everyone around might have this effect."

"No, it's just the way things worked out."

"You had better damn well know what you're doing. If anything goes wrong . . ."

"Are you threatening me, Sloan Hardt? Implying that I don't know my job?"

"Jesus, Cassidy. I'm sorry." He plunged a hand through his hair. "I'm lousy at emotional times like this."

Years of resentment reared its ugly head but she

squelched it ruthlessly. She needed to focus her energies on Montana. "Stay clear of Montana until you have yourself in a better place. The last thing she needs is your negative energy at a time like this."

"Stay away . . . ? You mean, I could be there if I want?"

"Yes. Just make certain it *is* what you want."

"Really? I never thought—"

"Why do you think she so desperately wants to have the baby at home? So anyone who wants to can be there. It's one of the things we discussed in preparation for this. Plus, she's hoping for as little medical intervention as possible. Doctors these days are pretty fast to pull out the scalpel."

"But what if something goes wrong? We're a long way from the hospital."

"Sloan, I know my job. Now butt out and let me do it." The trouble was, he was echoing her own thoughts far too closely for her comfort. She'd been well aware that the stimulation of the evening's festivities might stir things up and hoped it was the right thing.

She drew a deep breath and reminded herself she knew what she was doing. And that she was damn good at it.

"You're doing great, Montana. The baby's almost here. One more push ought to do it. Soon as you're ready."

Montana hung onto Steele with all her might as she pushed. For those waiting, it felt like a lifetime before the red, wrinkled face appeared, indignant at being forced from its comfy shelter.

"One more." Cassidy exhaled in a forced burst of air as

the shoulders appeared and finally the damp, warm newborn body slid into her waiting hands.

"A girl!" she announced, just as Her Highness started to squall.

She suctioned out the baby's mouth and nose and placed the infant on Montana's stomach, the umbilical cord still pulsing, as she waited for the placenta to make its appearance. "She's perfect," she told a triumphantly tired Montana. "She had it loads easier than you. Look how pink she is already."

Steele pushed a lock of sweat-dampened hair back from Montana's forehead. The look the two exchanged was so intimate, Cassidy felt a pang before she looked away. Luckily the placenta soon provided a great distraction.

She tied off the umbilical cord and handed Steele the scissors to do the honors. As Steele cut the cord, Cassidy glanced at Sloan. He appeared to be in shock, which was normal. At least he hadn't turned green or passed out. Steele had started to videotape the birth, but when things speeded up he'd shoved the camera into Sloan's hands.

Montana had a quick and uncomplicated birth. The baby was small but nicely plump, with good color and a high Apgar score. Cassidy felt Sloan's eyes on her as she moved away from the new parents, giving them the chance to form their new family. Helen took her cue from Cassidy as she wiped a few tears from the corner of her eye and hustled Zeb from the room.

Sloan hovered at Cassidy's side, wide-eyed with amazement. "Is it always like that?"

"She had a relatively easy time," Cassidy said. "She didn't even tear."

"I mean the way it feels. Like you just witnessed a miracle."

"Yeah." Cassidy smiled. "It's pretty much always like that."

"I had no idea before," Sloan said. "Now I understand why you do what you do."

"The whole experience is amazing. I love the way it brings the parents so close together, as they see the end result of what their love created."

"Yeah!" Sloan blew out a breath, as if he couldn't hold it all in.

"Montana told me one of the first things she wanted was a glass of champagne. Why don't you go do the honors?"

In no time she had the baby and mother both cleaned up, Montana in a pretty nursing nightie, the baby swaddled and happily snoozing before Sloan reappeared, champagne and glasses in hand.

"I thought you got lost. Out stomping the grapes?"

"I stopped to make a phone call," Sloan said.

"Your grandfather?" Cassidy asked.

"No. I left a message for my doctor. I canceled my vasectomy."

Cassidy's movements faltered for a moment before she recovered. "That's hardly a decision you ought to be making in the heat of the moment, Sloan."

With Helen and Zeb back on the ranch, Cassidy planned to vacate their suite. She didn't expect the opposition she received from Helen. "We'll be staying in Zeb's bungalow, dear. The suite is yours for as long as you want."

"But it's your suite, Helen. Your home forever."

The older woman smiled. "Forever is a long time. My son built this wing for me in a different lifetime, one I've moved on from. My place now is with my husband and he's not comfortable here in the ranch house."

Cassidy flopped down onto the bed. "How do you do that, Helen? How do you know when it's time to move on and just do it?"

"It's naturally easier when you have a partner by your side." She cocked her head. "I'm guessing perhaps you've outgrown West Bend?"

"It seems I can't accomplish the things I ultimately want to do there."

"Then I suggest you find someplace where you can."

"But how do you know, really know, this is the right place, the right time?"

"You must learn to act, not simply react. And to trust your instincts."

Cassidy frowned. "I don't get it."

"It's so much easier, so much safer, to simply react to others. Acting on your own, taking full responsibility, is much more difficult. But when you do, the rewards are huge. And they come from within."

A few days later, Cassidy started to pack her bag, only to be interrupted by Sloan, who seemed nonplussed to see her suitcase.

"I thought you'd be sticking around a little while longer."

Funny, since *he* hadn't been around since the birth. Without a word of explanation. "My work here is finished. It's time to get on with the rest of my life."

"Including Tony?"

"That's hardly your business."

"Don't go," Sloan blurted out. He caught her hand. "You know me so well. Better than anyone. I thought you'd understand what it meant when I canceled my vasectomy."

"I understand you were caught up in the moment. It happens to everyone."

"So get caught up in it with me. Stay a while longer at Black Creek. Give me a chance to prove myself. To woo you properly, the way you deserve."

Cassidy sighed. What she wouldn't have given to hear those words a short time ago.

"Sloan, everything has always come easily to you. But I'm not one of them."

He was silent for a moment. "If you're determined to go, I won't stop you. I'll even fly you back. But first there's something I need to show you."

"Sloan, there's absolutely nothing you can say or do—"

"Cassidy, I know you. I know you're fair. You'll give me this, or you'll angst forever if you don't."

Damn him, he *did* know her well.

"All right, then, I'll humor you. Only because it'll be much faster to have you fly me home."

He led her outside, then bundled her into a pickup truck.

"Did you ever hear the story about the Black Creek driveway?"

"I don't think so."

"Steele was trying to make a point with Montana, so when she was away for the day, he brought in excavation equipment and completely reconfigured the driveway. Before there had been two separate driveways: one to the spa, one to the ranch. After he was finished, it was all one."

"On her ranch! Wasn't she furious? I would have been."

"No, she understood what he was trying to say, the point he was trying to make."

"And what point are *you* trying to make?" They'd driven partway down the driveway, and Sloan switched to four-wheel drive as they jounced along what seemed like a cattle path before reaching a flat spot with the creek running through it.

He parked the truck, turned off the engine, and turned to her. "I went up to West Bend and looked at that house you want to buy."

"That was a waste of your time. The council refuses to change the zoning," she said flatly.

"I know. I bought the house anyway. It's a wonderful house and I could totally see why you fell in love with it."

"What on *earth* possessed you to do such a thing?"

"Temporary insanity?" That happy-go-lucky grin was back and she realized how much she'd missed it lately. Missed him.

"Even more insane, I've arranged to move it down here," he continued.

"Here, where?"

"Right here." He unrolled a blueprint and spread it on the truck seat between them. "I figure we'll set it here, so the deck faces east and catches the morning sun. We'll fence off the creek so the kiddies can't fall in and we'll turn this part of the yard into a playground. As an added bonus, any moms and kids who want can learn how to ride."

Cassidy felt her world spinning. Suddenly she couldn't breathe. Was she back on the Fantasy Cruise Line, about to wake up?

"Act," Helen had told her, "don't simply react," but she'd spent her entire life reacting and old habits were hard to break.

"What's all this 'we' stuff?"

"You've got a dream, Cassidy. I want to help you make it a reality."

"Playfair House is only a tiny part of it. What about the rest of my dreams?"

"I haven't finished building my house yet. We can add on another wing or another story. One with a nursery and whatever else you figure we'll need."

"What about your dreams?"

"Honey, if I can convince you to stay and give me a chance I don't deserve, making Black Creek Ranch the largest, most successful working dude ranch in the state will be a piece of cake. Especially with you by my side."

"Doesn't this land belong to Montana?"

"Nope, it's part of what I bought from her. Everything's legal and ready to go. That's what I've been doing these past few days."

"It sounds like you were pretty sure of me."

"Not for one single, solitary second. But I kept going back to that time in the barn, when we pricked our fingers and swore everlasting friendship."

"If you dare try to tell me this is all about being friends, I'll scream," she warned.

"Cassidy, I'm dense as hell, but I finally figured out there's a lot more between us than friendship. I love you."

Cassidy wrenched open her door, leapt out of the truck, and walked down to the creek. She could see it the way Sloan painted: the house, the playground. The children, playing with her and Sloan's children.

She heard him approach and turned to face him. As Sloan reached for her and took her into his arms, Cassidy realized he was trembling, not sure of her at all. Yet he'd done everything in his power to make her dream a reality.

"This is not the same as modifying a driveway, Sloan. I still need to do my work. It'll take me away part of the time."

"I know that. That's no problem."

"I'll probably need to get my pilot's license. And a small plane."

"Whatever you need. As long as it's okay with you that I need *you*."

"You were adamant about not wanting kids. This is a pretty sudden change of heart."

"My mom warned me that would happen, once I met the right woman. The night Saphera was born, I knew I wanted us to have a family together—to one day watch our kids playing with her."

"Oh, Sloan." She blinked back tears of happiness as she melted against him. "I'll want a second Playfair House in town, easily accessible to whoever needs it," she said. "This will be the retreat out here, vacation time or a getaway for those who couldn't otherwise manage it."

"Whatever you want, Cassidy. Together, we'll make it happen. So long as you never stop wanting me."

"I promise. And I love you, too, Sloan."

His tender kiss wrapped around her heart, cocooning her with all the love she could ever imagine feeling, forever.